ANIMAL HUSBANDRY

STORIES BY TAYLOR GARCÍA

ANIMAL HUSBANDRY

Copyright © 2024 Taylor García

Published by Unsolicited Press

Printed in the United States of America

First Edition

All rights reserved. No part of this book may be reproduced or transmitted in any form or by any means, electronic or mechanical, including photocopying, recording, or by any information storage and retrieval system without the written permission of the author, except where permitted by law.

This is a work of fiction. Any resemblance to actual events or persons, living or dead, is entirely coincidental.

Attention schools, libraries, and business: this title can be ordered through Ingram. For special sales, email sales@unsolicitedpress.com.

For information, contact:
Unsolicited Press
Portland, Oregon
www.unsolicitedpress.com
orders@unsolicitedpress.com
619-354-8005
Cover Design: Kathryn Gerhardt
Editor: S. Stewart
ISBN: 978-1-963115-32-1

Also by Taylor García

Slip Soul

Functional Families

For Jake Jones Hudson (PC 50) and Alfredo Guerra Jordan (PC 52)

"*My anaconda don't want none, unless my midget goat go get me some.*"

"*Here we go, Sancho!*"

R.I.P.

BID

He who makes a beast of himself

gets rid of the pain of being a man.

Hunter S. Thompson

CONTENTS

INTRODUCTION	15
THE VERMILLION BORDER	19
HUMBLY WE COME	41
JOURNEY TO THE EDGE OF THE EARTH	55
HERCULES MARTINEZ	71
CIRCLE OF DEATH	97
"CHAERONEA EVE"	113
ANIMAL HUSBANDRY	119
LIVED EXPERIENCE	149
WARPATH	163
THE BREAKFAST HOUSE	177
MEDICINE BOX	193
ONCE, A MAN	221

ANIMAL HUSBANDRY

STORIES BY TAYLOR GARCÍA

UNA VEZ, UN HOMBRE

Una vez,
Fui conejo
Inocente
Lindo
De vez en cuando
Travieso

Entonces,
Convertí en araña
Inteligente
Paciente
Sola
En mis hilos delicados

Más tarde,
Me cambié a perro
Juguetón, entrenado
Obediente, molestamente
Leal

Ahora,
Soy pájaro
Hábil
Intuitivo

Con alas, garras y pico
Listo para volar
Lejos

INTRODUCTION

A while back, I came across a writing contest asking for submissions about utopian futures. At first, I thought: "How wonderful an idea, to write about the ultimate outcomes, the stories with perfect endings." This thought was followed by, "It's an admirable goal, but my brain is more wired for dystopia." Then I thought, why? Why do I—and we humans in fact—tend to see what's wrong, or what could go wrong first, before we see what's positively possible?

For starters, we are in fact living in one of the most extraordinary times in human history and yet, we tend to be quite ungrateful for what we have. In times when we have access to immediate information, when human comforts and resources are relatively abundant, we are still somehow not satisfied. It's as if we're already living in a utopia, but we've decided to throw it all away, albeit gradually, because we likely know that life is pretty damn good, and could probably get a lot better, but our aptitude for destruction and pettiness gets in the way.

I believe the recent pandemic taught us that we are fragile human beings, and that something can indeed come along and destroy us if we aren't too careful. Humanity passed the pandemic hurdle, but did it really humble us? No. The world did not end, per se, we did not spiral into the apocalypse, but I believe it kicked off what was already in motion: the peri-apocalypse. The *middle times* of the apocalypse itself. Not pre, not post. *En medias res.*

This is what I mean by the gradual erosion and destruction of our humanity by our own negligence, apathy, and hubris. The pandemic was an appetizer.

So, why do we tend toward the slow death? If we know we can do something to right the ship, why don't we?

My other theory, is that the men on this planet, those humans born with male genitalia, those people who identify with the masculine gender, are going through their own identity understanding amidst all of this. The so-called decline, or perhaps reframing of the patriarchy, is just a slice of this masculine upheaval. This is in part why I often feel as though I am watching dystopia unfold piece by piece, and why I sometimes feel my kind—*man*-kind—has a lot to do with the demise. We male human animals are simply dealing with a massive shift in our identities, and the growing pains are real.

This story collection examines how the collective male identity has changed and continues to change as a result of global turmoil. It's about the evolution of males in a world that is no longer theirs, as they were once told it was. The men in these stories are doing what men are known to do: charge ahead, make things happen, carry what they believe is the world on their shoulders; however, they are not the men we once knew. These males are wandering into deeper, unknown waters. They are confronting their weaknesses and sometimes fighting them and sometimes giving into them. These men are also experimenting with a fuller spectrum of masculinity in their respective worlds. They are exploring beyond the male gender social norms that have pervaded and created what once was "A Man's World," and they are realizing that fighting is futile. They are weak as they are strong, honest as they are liars, incorrigible as they are redeemable. Something is changing, ending, dying in their individual worlds, and they are having to figure out how to make sense of it.

So, why men, why now, and why me?

1. Men are being asked to be and do differently, and we're struggling with it. We're realizing that inside each of us is a little boy, who once had intense emotions and passions that we didn't know how to reconcile, and we were taught to stuff them deep down inside like the men before us. We were taught to be macho, because there was no other way. But now, we're learning to channel our so-called strength beyond our biological wheelhouse: to protect, stand up, defend, and give voice to people, groups, and causes once thought to be unworthy for no other reason than they did not fit into the aforementioned Man's World. This means men are becoming more *hu-men*: progressing toward collaborative contribution and peaceful growth for the benefit and evolution of all humankind and eschewing the pre-programmed patriarchal machinations of aggressive gain and pointless competition.

2. It's long overdue. We're in the final act of pissing contests, which are getting quite old.

3. I was born male. I've never questioned the parts I was given. They make sense to me inside and out. I identify as male, as masculine, and I love being a man. And yet, I was also given bucket loads of emotion and intuition and sensitivity. I cry. Hard. I bottle up emotions, and I let them out. I'm incredibly loving and sweet, but I'm also rude, prone to aggression, and quite mean more

often than I want to be. I absolutely know I have a feminine side, because I believe in the duality of all things, and how I must be in touch with both sides of my persona to feel balance. I love and respect women, but I've also had my own hang ups about them. I admire and appreciate the female form and the immense range of emotion and compassion that comes with femininity, but I also often fear the fierceness and unpredictability of women. I've loved women, and I've also dreaded them. I am also intrigued by men and male energy. I've wanted to be like certain men, and I've also been curious about them sexually. I'm comfortable identifying as questioning on the spectrum of sexuality. I've always been questioning whether I am this or that. Some days it's this, others that. And I'm not mad at either. That's who I arrived as, the same way I once arrived with the male parts given to me.

This is the emerging new essence of man: the ability to understand and admit who we are inside and out, then transmute that into a positive energy we can share externally. That energy can and should be used for the good of others so that we contribute to the evolution of all humankind. By embracing, rather than fighting, by flowing rather than fixing, we might achieve the much-needed balance our planet, our hearts, and our species so desperately needs.

THE VERMILLION BORDER

Dear Elaine,

I'm going to miss your son Jay. He was my pledge brother when we joined the Delta Upsilon Kappa Fraternity at St. Mary's in the winter of 1996. Before we joined the fraternity, Jay and I were not close friends. We were more like distant acquaintances, friends of friends. But once we joined DUK, our bond started to form. As any one of my DUK brothers will attest, pledge ship bonds a group of strangers very quickly in an indescribable way. So, that's how Jay and I went from acquaintances to brothers.

We were both different people. Me, a Mexican-American from Las Cruces, New Mexico, and Jay, a blond pure Texan guy from Marble Falls, an area he so affectionately referred to as the Hill Country. With me being from New Mexico, I was always something of an outsider at St. Mary's. Jay made sure to remind me of that. He was, in fact, the one who dubbed my hometown, "Almost Mexico." He'd always attach that when describing me. He might have even called me "Almost Mexico" if I remember correctly!

Jay and I become really close during those years in San Antonio. We both took a Poetry class together. It was then that I realized that Jay was a fantastic writer. His poems had this strange and eerie and funny quality about them, all things that I love in writing. We often talked about stories we were going to write, or he would share ideas he had based on dreams or real (?) events from his youth. That was the fun and funny thing about Jay: he was always telling a tale, and you could never know if it was real or made up, but after a while, you realized that it was real, because that was the kind of man Jay was, always on the edge of things, always pushing boundaries, and challenging the conventional.

With Jay, I was able to push boundaries, too. I was always a good boy in high school, so when I arrived at college, I cut loose, and Jay became one of those partners in crime I never had. I knew he was a bad boy with a good boy past, just like me. I think all of us guys were, because we all took the fraternity, school, and our families very seriously. We were always there for each other.

Jay and I definitely got into our fair share of trouble together. I'll spare you some of those details, however, please know that even though we were up to no good much of the time, we always returned to our values, and we always managed to get ourselves out of trouble.

Post college, Jay came to stay with me in Santa Cruz, CA for a while. After St. Mary's, I moved back to New Mexico, but knew I wasn't long for it, so I moved to Santa Cruz in 2000, where I still am today. If I recall correctly, Jay arrived in Santa Cruz the summer of 2001, just shortly before 9/11. I'll never forget leaving for work that morning of 9/11, and Jay was there, waking up on the couch. He was already watching TV, and I paused to see the horror that was unfolding, but I still left to work, as though I was in a hurry. Back then, I always seemed to be in a hurry. I still am.

The Santa Cruz days were fun. We had a small posse of friends, plus, some of my relatives, and there were a couple of other St. Mary's alums in town, too. It was like we had a second college experience in liberal Northern California. Eventually, Jay moved back to Texas, said he had to take care of things back home. Over time, we mostly—unfortunately—fell out of contact. Nothing bad, no ill will, just a chapter closing, moving ahead and onward, becoming adults.

Jay and I kept in touch through the DUK network. We were trying to get all ten members of our pledge class to have a reunion in 2019 in Mexico City. Jay really wanted to do it, but he said he was having some health problems at the time. There was a lot of talk and promises from the other guys, but only about four of us made it. I wished there had been more times for us to reunite after college. Seems like yesterday we were all there at St. Mary's, but now we're all adults living in the real world. How I wish I could go back to those days.

Speaking of Mexico, I was just there a few weeks ago down in Mazatlán, when I received a funny meme from Jay via Instagram. It was some kind of La-Z-Boy recliner with army tank tires or something, and we were messaging about how we would both want that. I appreciated how he reached out. It was great to hear from him.

I hope and pray that his last few months and days were calm and easy for him, that he wasn't in any kind of danger or suffering. But I don't know, and I may never know. I know Jay had his own challenges in life, as we all do, and I often think about how much easier it would be for all of us to live only in a world where we put on our happy faces and ignore the problems. But I suppose that's the part of being an adult we have to contend with.

I'll leave you with one other tiny, funny, silly, and slightly gross memory. One night we were at the fraternity house. Must have been Paul Tran's house at the time. There was a party going on with loud music and groups of people talking, playing games, dancing, etc. All of this was going on, but Jay and I were just sitting on the couch watching TV. There were definitely some adult beverages involved, and who knows how far Jay and I were into said adult beverages. But I do remember we somehow both knew we had reached our limit. It was either something on TV, or maybe it was the noise from the party, but whatever it was, at one moment, Jay and I looked at each other and it was as if we had sent each other a telepathic message to get up and get out of the house ASAP. Something had turned our stomachs at the exact same time, and so the next thing we knew, he and I were both outdoors on the side of the house puking our guts out!

Okay, so, maybe that's not the most wholesome story to share, but it's one that sticks with me because it says something about our unspoken bond and the fun and strange times we had together.

Elaine, I am feeling so lost and sad about Jay's passing, and I hope you might soon find peace and light in this time of transition. I loved Jay, as all of us guys did, and we will miss him terribly. He will be remembered.

Enclosed are some photos from my personal collection, some copies of the DUK page from our yearbooks, plus two copies of his poems from the poetry class. I hope you enjoy them.

Please stay in touch (I have lots more photos!).

With light and love,
Abraham Vigil
"Almost Mexico"
Santa Cruz, CA

Dear Abraham,

Thank you for the letter and pictures. Your timing was perfect. Jay talked of you often, always with love and laughter. He thought the world of you. I appreciate you taking the time for handwritten correspondence. I don't deal much with email, and these days I'm not much for phone calls. I've been on the phone quite often talking about the circumstances surrounding Jay's death.

Jay died on August 4th in Mexico City. I received the call two days later from the local authorities there, and with the help of a translator, I found out that he was in a hotel in an area called Roma. You probably know more than I do about Mexico City, as you mentioned you and some of the guys went there a few years ago.

Getting Jay back to the United States was quite challenging. He's here now, and now the question is why he died. His blood had to be sent to the toxicology lab in Houston. The police said it will take nine weeks. I have eight weeks to go.

He wished to be cremated—found that in some papers he had left in his place here—and he had written that he wanted part of his ashes to be left in Mexico City. I don't know what I'll do when all of this is said and done. Next week is his cremation.

You can help me by letting your DUK brothers know that a service for Jay is not decided quite yet. If there is something, please know that all of you will be invited. As you may know, it was just Jay and me, since his father passed away years ago, and a few distant family members.

In closing, I may ask for your help once I receive his ashes to take a portion to Mexico City. I don't travel very far from my town, and though I would like to see that part of the world someday, it seems too remote of a possibility right now.

Lastly, do you know why Jay may have been so enchanted with Mexico City? He rarely talked about it, at least with me. The last time I saw him alive, he mentioned he was going to down to Mexico for a short vacation, but he didn't provide many details. I didn't know he was going to the city. I thought he was going to be on a beach somewhere. I recall you all have a fraternity brother in Mexico City? Perhaps that was his reason to visit?

Thank you again so much for your kindness.

Elaine Heath
Marble Falls, Texas

Dear Elaine,

Wow, where do I begin? First, thank you for the updates about Jay. I'm sorry to hear of the challenges to bring him home to the United States. I had read on a Facebook post that he was out of the country when he died—but I didn't know it was Mexico City exactly. No one else knew either.

About Mexico City, yes, we have a fraternity brother there, one of our pledge brothers, in fact. Rogelio "Gelio" Rodriguez. He currently lives near the Roma area. I don't know how much Jay and Gelio were in contact, but I believe not very much, because now that our DUK network is in contact about Jay's passing, Gelio said that he had not heard from Jay in a long, long time.

My thoughts about Jay's attraction to Mexico City is that he was very into Jack Kerouac, the beat generation writer. Jay was always talking about Kerouac's books and saying quotes and references from his writings. Kerouac wrote a book called *Mexico City Blues*. Kerouac lived there and wrote that novel. Well, it was poetry, actually. Your son was a good writer, and I know Kerouac inspired him quite a bit. Maybe he just wanted to be near the place where one of his heroes once lived, you know? I'm a forever fan of Gabriel García Márquez, and I know one day, I will go to Cartagena, Colombia to visit his final resting place.

About Jay's last wishes, absolutely yes. You have my word that I will help make that happen. I realize all these things take time, so please let me know when and how. I am sure you are dealing with so much right now.

Until next time,
Abe

Hello Abe,

I now have Jerry's ashes. I don't know if I can let go of him just yet. When it's time, I'll let you know. I will have to think of how I might get some of them to you to take to Mexico City. With you in California and me in Texas, that might be complicated. Any ideas?

I've had some time to sort through the papers and belongings in Jay's place. I came across several journals and papers, some handwritten, some typed, with his writings. He never really shared a lot of that with me, with our family. I knew he liked to write and was studying English at St. Mary's. Seeing and reading this all now, I feel like I'm getting to know a new side of him. It's very sweet, and it also makes me sad knowing that he kept this to himself.

You were right about his affinity for Jack Kerouac. I found some printouts of Jack Kerouac poems, and then right behind it was something Jerry had written. I could tell he was trying to imitate his style. It was cute to see that.

I wanted to ask you something. In your first letter, you shared a silly (and disgusting!) story about you and Jay. Would you mind sharing more of those anecdotes? I don't care if they are silly, or disgusting, or both. It doesn't matter to me. I'd like to know more about what you boys were really up to in those days. Would you please?

Thank you again,
Elaine Heath

Dear Elaine,

You mentioned the poems of Kerouac followed by his poems. I remember that exercise in our poetry class! Our professor, Sue something, had us find our favorite poet or poems and asked us to write in their style to master the pacing and tempo. She always reminded us that poetry was simply music in its base form—just beats and bits of lyrics. Jay was really good at that. He could read something and then write something that matched it. Sue was always having him read his poems in class, which always got everybody's attention because, while the girls were writing about lemon merengue pie and love (or me writing about the goddamned Spice Girls) Jay was writing about the soy refinery plant in town and the local crack heads. He had a keen eye for what was really going on just outside of our bubble. It's like he knew danger was everywhere.

You asked me to share more stories about our college shenanigans. I admit I'm a bit afraid/embarrassed—not sure what—to share, but you asked, so here's a couple.

One of my fondest memories is surrounding that Poetry class. Jay, me and Jeremiah, one of our closest fraternity brothers who was one year ahead of us, took that class together. It was every Thursday at 1:30 pm. Thursday at 1:30 pm is a tempting time of the week. It's when a lot of kids started skipping classes to start their weekend debauchery. Plus, Thursday night was known as International Party Night—not sure why it was called that, but you could always find a party on Thursday night.

Anyway, even though it was a Thursday afternoon, Jay, Jeremiah, and I still made it to Poetry class. Jay usually worked right up until that time, and I was either in the cafeteria or coming from my dorm, and Jeremiah was arriving at the college since he lived off campus. Early on we established this ritual where Jay would pick us up in his truck near the cafeteria and drive us to the other side of campus to the Language Arts building. He would pull up blasting Pearl Jam—he loved Pearl Jam—and we would hop in prepared for an adventure. It was all of about a five-minute drive, most likely less, but we somehow maximized that very short trip.

How did we maximize that short trip? Well, Mrs. Heath, if you didn't already know, your son, as well as all the other DUK's were massive stoners. Potheads. Reefer addicts. You asked, so I'm telling… Jay always had something to smoke for Jeremiah and me on that short ride. A joint, a pipe, a pinch hitter, a blunt. I don't know if we ever arrived at that class in our right minds not reeking of smoke.

One time, Jay didn't have any grass or at least anything rolled up or in a pipe. He asked Jeremiah to rifle through the glovebox of Jay's truck. Magically, in the crevices and corners of the glove box, under car registration paperwork and fast food napkins, there was just enough loose weed and other stuff—most likely dust or dried resin or tobacco or whatever—that Jay managed to stuff into a pipe, which we then smoked. Who knows what we were smoking?? Whatever it was, it did the trick. We caught some kind of a high.

I feel so embarrassed to share that. I hope it doesn't come as a shock to you.

We also did a lot of pranks. I mean A LOT. Once, we decided to stick a bottle of dish soap in a water fountain outside the Student Union Building. We cut the top off the bottle and just sat in in the middle of the fountain in the dark of night. By the morning, the whole thing was bubbling over into the courtyard and all over the sidewalks. It was like a police scene with security trying to close off the area, while the custodial staff tried to clean it all up.

Maybe I should stop there. I would hate to paint a bad picture about Jay, may he rest in peace.

Once again, please let me know if I can help in any way.

Kind Regards,
Abe

Dear Abe,

Oh dear, I knew about Jay and all his "habits." It's true, he was a good boy in high school, but by the end of it, he started "experimenting" and then went off to college, where I can only imagine the fun you all had and the trouble you got into. And I knew he liked to smoke weed. That was no secret. I mean, I'm a child of the 1960's, so you can imagine what we were up to back then.

At any rate, please keep the stories coming. Good or bad, or sad. It doesn't matter.

Here's a funny one for you. Once, Jay had an apartment near our home in Marble Falls—it was during the college years—and we had some distant cousins in town from Louisiana. I had let them stay in Jay's apartment for a few nights. I think Jay was due home for the summer soon. Anyway, my cousin's little girl, she was about five years old, happened to find a huge bong in Jay's kitchen he had hid under the sink. It was a hideous thing. It was the head of a shark that was gritting its teeth and it was smoking a cigar I believe. And it was huge! The little niece thought it was a toy or something because she was playing with the bowls and things. Oh gosh, I had to have a little talk with Jay after that.

Well, in other news, I have received the toxicology report. I'm going to keep that to myself for now. I want to continue to think about my happy memories of Jay. I'm still holding on, and you know what, I may never let go. I'm sure all your DUK brothers are anxious for answers and want to know how and when I might put him to rest, but it's just hard. I think you know Jay's father passed away when you boys were in school, so it's just been Jay and I all these years. You never think you will outlive your children.

Thank you again, Abe, for your time.

Kindly,
Elaine

Elaine,

I completely understand. Take your time. These are all very private matters. I was looking through a box of pictures I have from the St. Mary's days and wow, I realized how young we actually were. We were kids. I look at myself now, and I feel like such a tired old adult. I'm on my second marriage that isn't going so well. I have a teenage daughter who disowned me after my first marriage broke up, and my stepson with my current wife is now questioning whether they are a *boy*. They're a *they* now. My company is downsizing and there's talk that our division will reduce by ten percent. I doubt I'll have a position here soon. I don't know which way the world is going. I don't know if we're on the cusp of something really truly great, or if this is the beginning of the end. The real end.

I hate to be so gloomy and sad all of a sudden, but all those pictures, all the memories are flooding back in, and it makes me realize that we should just follow those dreams we had as kids. I wanted to be an archeologist and go discover hidden caves with artifacts, then share about them in National Geographic as a renowned explorer. Now, I get excited for a two-night sales meeting in Palm Springs.

I know I shouldn't complain to you. I know I should consider myself lucky, which I do, so I will stop. Thank you for letting me share and vent.

I'll share another story. It's somewhat controversial. A deep secret. Once, Jay and I were driving back to campus from a party. We had just picked up some greasy food from Jack in the Box, and we passed this big fancy house that always dressed up their lawn with whichever holiday it was. It was Easter time and this house had an over-the-top display with bunnies and ducks and eggs and stuff. I was joking that I always hated Easter and the Easter bunny because I was traumatized by it as a kid. My parents took me to one of those mall Easter Bunny picture places, like Santa, and they sat me on the bunny, but because the bunny looked evil, I screamed and peed my pants. It remains a very popular Vigil family story.

Anyway, Jay said, "Well, let's go show that fucking bunny who's boss."

He pulled over and we jumped out. I don't know what we were going to do, but we were going to do something. There was one bunny, the Easter Bunny itself, in the middle of their display.

"That one," Jay said.

And so we went for it. It was about six feet tall, an old school plastic thing that lit up. It wasn't heavy, but it needed two sets of hands to move it, which we were doing without even talking about it. We lifted it from the yard, threw it in the bed of Jay's truck and took off. We laughed all night, brought it to the DUK house, and everybody had a blast with it. Over the next few weeks, it became the centerpiece of the house. People took pictures with it, danced with it, it held beer cans, someone carved a whole in the mouth and stuck a cigar in there. Someone dressed it in one of our DUK jerseys. You name it, we defiled it. Jay and I were pretty proud of it.

Then, it all came crashing down because someone knew where it came from. It turned out that house was the home of a San Antonio city councilwoman whose niece went to St. Mary's. The niece had come to a DUK party around that time, she noticed the bunny immediately, and then word spread fast. No social media in those days, but the phone lines lit up. That family tried to come after the DUK's and the college, but thank god we had a local alum who was an attorney who said that nothing could be proven in a court of law. We had to destroy everything though. All the pictures, etc. No one spoke a word.

But Jay, being a good guy at heart, said he was going to take care of the bunny since he was the one who provoked it. He took it and said he threw it at the dump. We never saw it again, and over time, things settled down. The Councilwoman and her family eventually gave up on harassing us. It was awful for a while.

Well, I suppose that wasn't the best story either, and now I've portrayed us, Jay, as not only drinking, pot smoking hoodlums, but also criminals. I'm sorry. I'm closer to fifty years old and I can't believe I'm sharing all this stuff.

I should close for now. Jay was a great man. He always put his friends—our brotherhood—first. He would do anything for us. He always wanted to make us laugh, and he did.

Until next time,
Abe

Abe,

Ah, the bunny story. Yes, I knew all about it. And guess what? That damn bunny is still in his garage here in Marble Falls. He never let go of it. I was reading your last letter filled with sadness and joy because he held onto it after all those years. That must have been one of his fondest memories. I agree, it was pretty bad what you two did, but that's what kids are supposed to do. Be kids. It sounds as though you have matured a lot since then, and I'm sure sharing that story felt good to get off your chest.

And please don't worry about sharing what's going on in your life. It's okay to share. We all have problems and challenges. That's how life goes. I hate to tell you, but it doesn't get any easier. It just keeps going and going but over time you learn how to come back from the sad and challenging times with ease and strength.

I wanted to share this with you. I found it in some papers of Jay's. It's a poem.

What to do
What to do

We're just babies, man
We're just babies

That's not your mother,
That's a man, baby

A man,
Baby

A baby man

That's who I am
I don't know what I would do
Contemplate
A state of debate

This life or the next?
Handle me with care

Please

I only want peace

There's more, and I can send them. This one stood out though. It was fairly recent. It also reminded me that when I received the call from the Mexican authorities, they said that Jay had several personal effects, including papers and books, a typewriter, and a roll of paper that had a lot of words on it.

When you go there, perhaps you can collect them and send them to me? But with one condition: Please only collect the good things. I don't want to have anything that might make me think of any harm to my son. I know all you boys had your vices and addictions and worries and anxieties and health problems and what have you, just like Jay did, and I suppose there is a place for all those, but at this point, let's leave them where they lie.

I have learned that I can send a portion of his remains via US Priority Mail. May I send that to you soon? But also know that I don't expect you to make that trip immediately. Only go when it's convenient for you. Enclosed is a note with the additional information about where you can collect his things. Please let me know when you have a moment.

Regards,
Elaine

Dear Elaine,

I've been thinking a lot about what you said about our vices and worries and health problems. I knew that Jay had something going on with his health even back in college. One time he shared with me and Jeremiah that he had passed blood in his urine and back then we all kind of made a joke out of it. We used to make this joke that when we partied too hard we had to "puke and rally," or sometimes we had to "piss and rally." As in, do our business and get back into the fun. I know, this is not funny, not then, not now. I remember telling Jay he should go get that checked out. And I think he did. He was out of school for a long time our junior year, but when he came back, he made nothing of it and wanted all of us to make nothing of it either. He didn't tell anybody what happened or why he was gone. In those days, we all seemed to know each other's business and we always supported each other through whatever was going on. But this was different. Jay wanted it to be his matter only, and so we didn't pry. It's like I said in my first letter to you: I just hope that he wasn't suffering or hurting in any way up until his last days. I just wish I had done a better job of keeping in contact with him. I feel like in staying in touch with you, I am attempting to fix that, and if anything, working to keep his memory alive.

So, yes, please Mrs. Heath, send his remains, and I will be more than happy to place at least part of him in Mexico City as he wished. I promise to write to you from there.

Sincerely,
Abe

Dear Elaine,
Writing to you from Mexico City

I would like to inform you that Jay's remains arrived at my home in Santa Cruz with no problems. When I saw the box that said "Human Remains," I nearly lost it. I could not believe that I was holding my brother in the palm of my hands like that. During our rallies as pledge brothers, Jay and I used to stand side by side because we were the same height. Holding him there, it felt like those moments on those cold winter nights when we were pledging allegiance to Delta Upsilon Kappa. I booked my flights to Mexico soon after and made arrangements to meet our brother Rogelio Rodriguez.

Gelio and I had just the place to set Jay's ashes. There's a park called Plaza Luis Cabrera. It's in a section of Mexico City called Cuauhtémoc, the namesake of the last Aztec emperor. It is said that Jack Kerouac went to that plaza to lay in the grass while he was on a peyote trip. Gelio and I thought it was an appropriate place to put Jay to rest. It's a charming small section of the city with cafes and shops. There's even a Starbucks there. I suspect that Jay probably spent some time at that plaza while in Mexico City.

We collected his things, and you're right, there was a roll of paper with hundreds, if not thousands of words on it. That's how Jack Kerouac used to write; he had an endless roll that he added to daily in a stream of consciousness. There were a few interesting things, too. Some Mayan souvenir trinkets, some old pictures, looked like family pictures, one that seemed like one of Jay and his dad with some miniature goats. Jay was always talking about miniature goats. We never knew whether those were real or not.

Gelio decided to keep all the other stuff like the typewriter and books in a box. The rest of it was mostly receipts and scribbles and some old hats and clothes, cigarette boxes, and lighters. Don't worry, there was nothing there that indicated harm.

All over Mexico City, there are these little encased shrines in the most unsuspecting places. Some of them have saints or statues of the Virgen de Guadalupe, others have rosaries, dead plants, pictures of people, burning candles. Maybe someone died there, or experienced a miracle, or just felt that spot was a spiritual place. There happened to be one there in the Plaza in an old flowerbed. It's hard to tell if anyone takes care of those little altars since they seem left to time. Gelio and I placed Jay's ashes inside that shrine. He's safe now, and if you ever visit, I'll let you know how to get there.

Enclosed here is a portion of a poem that he seemed to be working on.

<u>The Vermillion Border</u>

Here, in the land of
Canola oil and corn
Is a man

His solace is neither
Here nor there

In between
Life and death

Where everything is nothing
And nothing is everything

Where no harm
Will foul the flesh

Separated by a border
A demarcation so
Sharp
That it could kill

Yet so gentle that it could
    Kiss
    You on the lips

Guarantee your trip
To heaven
On some days
Hell on others

Not quite red
Nor orange
Not blood
Nor plasma

Miasma

Left behind by the
Shade of time

Never to be returned again
Such is best
Time to rest

Thank you so much for letting me help shepherd Jay to where he wanted to be. It has been my distinct honor.

Sincerely,
Abraham Vigil

Dear Abraham,

I'm sitting here writing to you from Marble Falls, Texas, the place of my birth and the birth of my son, Jay Heath. I have with me the rest of Jay's ashes. I am keeping them in a small urn on a shelf alongside some family pictures. There's one of Jay and his father, I believe on the same day or around the same time as the picture of the miniature goats you referenced. That was a family friend that raised those, and Jay loved them. He loved to feed them and talk to them. He begged us for one when he was little. How darling is that? I think he always wanted a little brother or sister. A little playmate, or as you said, a little partner in crime. That's why I'm so thankful he found all of you guys. I cannot tell you how much he loved the brotherhood and the things you all did together. It was probably some of the best times of his life. Thank you for being part of it. I'm ready to share that the toxicology report showed that he died of natural causes. Yes, he was on his multiple medications, but those were all within normal ranges. He was a private man, and I didn't know that his illness had progressed so much. It was a rare disease he had, one that breaks down the red blood cells. I don't know if you knew that. His prognosis was good for a long time, but things like that can turn; I know his did. I think he was trying to be strong and not worry me. I know he had said once that he might go to Mexico to get a procedure to help with the illness, but now that I know he was trying to live out on of his life's dreams—to be where his hero Jack Kerouac once wrote—I'm just happy he achieved what he wanted.

In closing, I wanted to ask if you might help with one more thing. I know I've asked you for so much. Might you help me find where I can send in his writing? Maybe a publisher or an agent somewhere. I suppose it's one way this mother might help keep her son's spirit alive. Please let me know if you can help with that.

With love,
Elaine Heath

HUMBLY WE COME

I.

Their collection plates were fuller this week, bigger bills, like twenties and tens. It went like this, especially in the run up to Easter and Christmas. People were more generous in the springtime, and more so in December. How people simply emptied their wallets and pocketbooks at this one moment each week was what kept the guys going—they'd always have a job to do.

Ron, with his always fuller basket collected from the nave, whispered the same thing every time to Graig and Tomás, who came from the wings with theirs, when they met at the back of the congregation to pour it all into the larger basket.

"You guys want take your cut?" Ron said.

They'd laugh about it later every time, remark how much cash it was, and how they could easily grab a handful without anyone ever noticing. No one paid attention to that final batching of funds, not even the priest.

"No, I'm serious," Ron brought it up again at Cass St. Bar, their Sunday evening tradition. "I really think we should. They don't count that shit until the next day. They'd never know."

"You're going to steal?" Tomás said. "From the church?"

"It's not from the church. When the cash goes from people's pockets into those baskets, it's not the church's money…yet." Ron drained his bottle of Miller Lite.

"He has a point," Graig said.

"I can't believe you fuckers are that desperate for money," Tomás said.

"I'm joking. You guys know I'm joking." Ron raised his hand, ordering another beer.

"Remember this place back in the day?" Graig surveyed the room, shook his head.

"Good ole' Mass, Cass, and Ass." Ron whistled.

"Remember after the Singles Cruise, we came here with those girls and Tomás got so shitfaced he threw up on the shuffleboard table?" Graig laughed, reaching for Ron.

"After fifteen years, will you ever say my name correctly, güey? It's To-MÁS. Not Toe-moss."

"Don't change the subject, cabrón," Ron said.

"Now, that's how you pronounce Spanish," Tomás said, punching Graig's bicep. "And that's what you are, a cabrón."

"His Irish ass no speaka," Ron said.

"So, then how does a chino like you have such a good accent?" Tomás said.

"Because I'm brown," Ron said. "Like you."

"You're not brown, you're yellow," Graig said.

"Listen to this white guy, assigning our colors. I'm offended," Tomás said.

"Well, at least I'm not stealing from the collection bins," Graig laughed.

"Yeah, Susan must be taking him for all he's worth," Tomás laughed, looking to Graig for a supportive chuckle.

But it pierced them all, stinger like. The barb still stuck in the skin. Ron lunged at Tomás. Graig held him back.

"You shut the fuck up, okay?" Ron spat at Tomás.

"I'm sorry—I knew that was wrong. I'm so sorry."

"Too fucking soon," Graig said.

"I know, I know. I'm sorry." Tomás extended a hand to Ron.

Ron refused at first, shook his head, biting his lip, reaching for the new sweaty brown bottle awaiting him. He swigged, turned back to the guys.

"You don't know what fuck I'm going through. I'm losing everything. My family, my kids, my money." Ron's eyes welled up. He was the ugly crier of the three. Graig leaned over, threw his big arm around Ron. Hushed him.

"It was fucked up what I said," Tomás said. "I'm really sorry. I know it's tough."

"Do you?" Ron swung around from the bar. "Do you? What do you know? Perfect fucking marriage."

"Shit, my marriage isn't perfect. No marriage is. You know we're in counseling." Tomás said.

"Look at us, whining like a bunch of bitches," Graig said.

"You're the only that's figured it out," Ron said to Graig. "Hitting fifty and still not married."

"It's not all it seems. I've told you guys that," Graig said. "Let's get going. This place is D-E-A-D, dead."

"Like my sex life," said Tomás.

"So, that's what's up?" Ron said.

"That's how it starts," Tomás said.

"Who says?" Ron said.

"Father McPartlin."

"The priest is telling you that?" Graig said.

"Well, not in those words. In counseling, Father says Monique and I have to touch each other at least sixteen times a day. No touching, means no playing. His words," Tomás said

"I don't know if I'd be taking advice from a celibate old white guy. Probably in the closet," Ron smirked.

"Let's go, guys. I need to get home," Graig said.

"Home to what?" Ron said. "Come on, you guys. Help a brother out."

"One more round." Graig waved his finger in a circle above his head. They settled in.

II.

The following Sunday, rain poured all morning over Pacific Beach, cleared by the afternoon, and left a cool gray halo for the five o'clock mass. The guys arrived by 4:40 to gather their supplies, huddle up, check in with the pastors, pray. The ushering was the easy part. It was the waiting for their big job—the gathering and bringing of the gifts—that was the most difficult. All the waiting. Once, they had devised an abbreviated mass: Greetings, Gospel, Host, Ghost; as in, get your wafer and ghost. They'd eliminate half the clergy and work themselves out of a job. But who cared, it wasn't a real job anyway.

At the back of the church, pouring their respective booty into the tall basket, Ron whispered, this time, "Cass St?" An inquiry. Graig never needed convincing. Tomás was always the one that needed to look up a bit, tilt his head side-to-side, check his mental calendar, make sure he had whatever kind of permission he needed before he nodded yes. He always nodded yes. It was the second Sunday of Advent. Why the hell not?

Cass was busier than usual. There were young people. Church goers, like the old days.

"I guess the tradition is picking back up," Graig said, peeling off his sport coat.

"Some pretty girls here," Ron said.

"Yeah. Yeah." Tomás said. He was somewhere else. He had shook his head "no" to the bartender on the first round.

"You guys sticking around for Christmas?" Graig said.

"Yeah, kids are coming to my place for Christmas Eve, then Susan's for Christmas Day. I don't know what I'm going to do."

"Let's hang out," Graig said. "I'm just going up to Riverside to my sister's place for Christmas Eve, but I'll be back late that night. I can't stay too long at her place. Her fucking kids. What about, you Toe-moss?"

"We're going down to Tecate. Monique's aunt wants us over. She thinks this will be her uncle's last Christmas. He's not doing well. The COPD. He caught that recent strain of Covid and still hasn't bounced back."

"Fuck, well, cheers." Ron held up his bottle, Graig his glass, Tomás his fist.

"I think I'm going to bounce, guys," Tomás said. "Monique wants me home. She just texted. She wasn't feeling well after mass."

"All good," Graig said.

"Seriously, you're a lucky man," Tomás said.

"Yeah. Some days," Graig said, looking away. "What do you guys want to do for Super Bowl?"

"Too far away," Ron said.

"See, you can plan that far ahead," Tomás said. "We can't."

"Okay, yeah, so that's where I'm lucky," Graig laughed.

"You ever hear from Tracy?" Ron said.

"Old news. She kind of fizzled out," Graig said.

"That's how all of yours end, huh? The old fizzle out." Tomás sat back down on the barstool.

"It's the most convenient." Graig shrugged.

"Every marriage should have a fizzle out option. Once it fizzles out, you two can just part ways. No courts, no judge." Ron tilted his beer back into his mouth.

"Shit, every man in the country would sign up for that," Tomás said. "So, you getting back into the scene, or what?"

"I thought you were leaving?" Graig said.

"Shit, okay, I guess I'll go. Just asking. I have a few minutes anyway." Tomás tapped his phone.

"Well, get a beer, bitch." Graig lifted up his glass.

"So, are you?" Tomás said.

Graig leaned into the bar, flagged the bartender, and ordered for Tomás.

"Yeah, are you?" Ron said.

"I don't know. I'm just kind of taking a break," Graig said.

"A dating break?" Ron said.

"Yeah, just a break." Graig shrugged.

Tomás' drink arrived.

"Drink up, buttercup," Graig said, raising his glass.

"A break. This guy," Ron said.

"Yeah, what the fuck, you guys? I'm just focusing on me for a while."

Ron and Tomás burst into laughter.

"Bro," Tomás said, "last time I checked, you've been focusing on yourself for like fucking ever."

"Shit, you guys. See, this is why we can't be friends." Graig laughed. "You just don't know how to hang with a bachelor."

"More like the golden bachelor," Ron laughed. "But, wait, wait, wait. Seriously. Why the break?"

Graig looked into his drink, shaking the glass, the ice clinking around. He laughed a bit.

"You guys," he said.

"No, that's okay if you are," Ron said.

"If I'm what?" Graig puffed up.

"Nothing. I was just asking why." Ron held his hand up, about to tap Graig on the chest.

"I thought you were implying—" Graig said.

"I wasn't implying anything. Now *you're* the one implying something."

"Guys, just shut up, okay? Leave it," Tomás said, eyeing Ron. "I get it. He's taking a break. Don't you get it, Ron?"

"Yeah, yeah, it's fine. I get it," Ron said.

They drank. Tomás stayed for another round, and then another. He wasn't in a rush after all.

III.

Sunday next, the temperature had dropped considerably though the sun had shone bright all day. Then, as was typical for the West Coast during Daylight Savings Time, night fell fast and hard at 5 p.m. Graig and Ron were on time, Tomás—nowhere to be seen. Mass was starting at 5:30 pm that night due to a nativity scene photo shoot in the nave. Even St. Brigid's believed in the magic hour. The church was already filling up because many parishioners forgot the 30-minute delay. Graig and Ron began ushering right when they arrived, having little time to prep, or chat. Still no Tomás.

On a trip back to the main doors, Graig tilted his chin up to Ron.

"Any word from T?"

Ron waved Graig to come closer so he could say something in his ear. Graig leaned in.

"He's in the right wing. Over by the organ. He's kneeling. Praying. When I went toward him, he waved me off, and his face was a mess. He's been crying."

"Seriously? What's going on?" Graig said.

"I don't know. He wouldn't say."

"Is he ushering tonight?"

"I don't know. You can go ask, but it looks like he doesn't want to be bothered," Ron said.

"It's weird he's actually praying," Graig said.

"I know. Something's up."

"Monique stuff?" Graig said.

"Yeah. Must be."

Tomás joined them right before the collection. He filed in, picked up his plates, nodded to Graig and Ron, his eyes bloodshot, his whole person trying to contain whatever it was that was tearing him apart. At the money dump, the one moment each week where they met without alcohol for their most solemn job, the beats passed quickly. Ron's opportunity to ask them to beers, which happened right before they walked up the aisle, came and went. No eye contact amongst the three of them. Aside from *Humbly We Come* rising from the organ's pipes and Connie's shrill voice accompanying it, only Tomás' soft shudders filled their small procession.

At the back of the church, with plates and baskets stowed until the next week, Ron had to ask. He held up his right hand in front of his sternum, pantomiming a glass mug, and gave a quick shrug of his shoulders. Graig was in. Always. Tomás, with very little deliberation, was an emphatic yes.

They took a table at Cass. A rare thing. And they ordered food. Another rare thing. Nachos, tater tots. They only nibbled against the two rounds that went down faster than usual under a subdued silence, interspersed by forced observations of the basketball, football, and surfing on the TVs around them. Tomás had calmed by then, his face tired more than anything, the lines from his nose to mouth somewhat deeper, weighed down by his frown.

"Look, man, whatever's going on, you can talk to us about it," Ron said.

"Or not. If you need us to just be here for you, that's fine, okay?" Graig said.

"Yeah, that, too." Ron waited for Tomás.

Tomás breathed in, and breathed out, the whoosh of air from his lungs poured out over the center of the table, onto their food and drink, flood like. He'd given his body permission to let go, to let it out.

"Thanks, guys." He exhaled again, looked up to the ceiling, then back at them. "I'm just going to tell you guys, okay? I had other kids. I mean, I have other children. Monique's not their mother. They're two girls back in New Mexico. Grown kids."

"Oh. Wow." Ron said. "Does Monique—"

"She does now," Tomás said.

Graig sat back in his chair, whistled.

"Yeah. In counseling, we had to tell everything. All our secrets. All the lies we've told. The crushes, affairs. Everything. And, so I did. I told her everything."

"And did that help?" Graig said.

"Uh, no," Tomás said. "But the priest said it's supposed to. I don't even know why the fuck I still follow this fucking crap."

"So, these kids—your other children—do you know them?" Ron said.

"No. They don't know anything about me either. Until now. Their mother, my ex-girlfriend from like a hundred years ago just messaged me out of nowhere…"

Tomás' voice began to cave. His chin quivered and his face screwed up.

"I mean, I knew I had them—that we had them—but I just fucked up, and Lisa—my ex, she pushed me out of their lives when they were little, and I wanted out anyway because I wasn't ready either, so they didn't know me. They never knew me. Some other dude raised them. After a while, I just stopped trying and so I forgot about them. Then I moved to California and met Monique, and well…"

"The rest is history." Graig laid his hand on Tomás's shoulder.

"But that's not all," Tomás looked up them. His trembling chin gave way to his suddenly gaping mouth, trying to breathe, but also gushing with sobs, his eyes scrunched and wet with tears again. "The younger one, my second daughter—Melanie—she's dying. She's got cancer. It won't be much longer. She's only 17-years-old."

Ron and Graig said nothing. Tomás' guttural cries got the attention of a few Cass St. patrons, including their server, who came to check on them. Graig waved her off, shook his head. She left a fresh stack of napkins anyway.

"I don't know what to do," Tomás said. He grabbed one of the napkins, wiped his eyes and blew his nose.

"What does Monique say?" Ron said.

"She's still in shock about the whole thing. I just told her about my other family last week. She doesn't know about the one that's dying. I found that out this morning. The timing of all this is—I don't know. It's unbelievable. And to answer your question, Monique's even more distant. I don't know how much longer we're going to last."

"What about the other mom? Lisa? Does she want you there?" Graig said.

"I don't know. Yeah? I guess. She treats me like she did back then. Like trash. Her DM on Facebook was something like, 'You should probably know that your daughter is dying.' I just don't know what to do. I feel like—like killing myself."

"Stop it," Ron said. "Just stop. Don't talk like that. You have to go there. You have to be there. She's your daughter. She's your flesh and blood."

"But what about my family? What are they going to do? The kids don't even know about my other kids," Tomás said. "What's going to happen when all these people find out about it? All these gossiping church assholes. My work, my clients?"

"They're just going to deal with it," Graig said. "And fuck them if they can't handle it, you know?"

"Yeah, you have to take your family with you. They need to know, too" Ron said.

"It's not that easy, guys. My family will freak out. My kids won't even know how to process this. They're young."

"They'll bounce back. Kids are resilient. My kids were destroyed at the beginning of our shit," Ron said, "but now they're in the new routine. They figure it out."

"But this isn't a divorce, dude. I mean, there probably will be a divorce. And then I'll have to face Lisa and her family and my older daughter—oh shit, I haven't seen her...since she was a toddler."

"You have to do it," Graig said. "You have to tell them."

"Wow, look at you, Mr. Face-The-Music." Ron harumphed, tipped his head back.

Graig pushed his drink aside. He began touching his nose, eyes dodging them both.

"What is it?" Tomás said. "You got kids somewhere, too?"

Graig stared ahead, his face serious, his shoulders squared.

"I couldn't say it last week, but I'm ready now. I'm taking a break...from women."

"Aw, buddy, we knew you were gay," Tomás said.

"No," Graig said. "That's not it. And what do you mean, you knew I was gay?"

"We kind of knew you were—different," Ron said. "Guys who stay single their whole lives—"

"Are fucking smart," Tomás said.

"No, I'm not," Graig said. "I finally figured it out. I'm asexual. I don't like women. Never really have. Or men. It just hit me."

"But you're happy?" Tomás said.

"I guess," Graig said. "I'm happy I figured it out. I feel better somehow. But this isn't about me right now. It's about you. You're going to get through this. We're going to be there for you. We'll go with you, won't we, Ron?"

"Dude, my head is spinning," Ron said. "Over here I've got papa-was-a-rolling-stone and over here I've got No-Nuts-Ned."

Graig socked Ron on the arm. "I still have testicles, you asshole."

"No, I'm fucking joking. It takes balls to share what you just did. Bravo for sharing that, G. It must feel good to get that off your chest. And he's right, T, we're going to be with you, bro. Every step. Every single step."

"I fucking love you guys," Tomás said. "It's weird, I've known you guys for years, but I've never really *known you* known you. Like Graig, bro, it's fine. You're going to be fine, okay? You can be whoever you want."

Ron shook his head. Looked into his drink. "You know, I've done some horrible things in my life. Stuff my mother, my wife—now ex-wife—my kids would disown me for. But for all those bad things, I keep trying to do good things, you know. You're a good man, Tomás, remember that. And you, too, G. It doesn't matter who or what you are."

The server came back to check on them. She approached them with a cautious smile.

"You guys okay?"

"Yeah, we're fine," Tomás said. "One more?"

"Why the hell not?" Graig said.

The server walked away. A comfortable short, silence fell over them. The bar, dressed in holiday lights began to fill up. Ron reached into his coat pocket and pulled out some bills. He laid a fifty-dollar bill on the table.

"I'll get this one," he said.

Graig and Tomás shared a look. They tried to wind down the smiles that were growing on their faces.

"What?" Ron said.

"Seriously?" Graig said.

Tomás laughed. He laughed so hard, the laughs went silent, turning to something of a physical cackle until he was in actual tears, that combination of laughter and sadness that feels like the solar plexus coming unstitched.

"Dude, are you okay?" Graig reached for Tomás.

Ron stood from his seat, about to come over to him.

Tomás waved his finger, the crying subsiding, the laughter returning.

"Who—" Tomás caught his breath, wiped his eyes with the cuff of his dress shirt. "Who in the fuck lays a fifty in the collection plate?"

Graig drank, shrugged his shoulders, and turned to Ron.

"Fuck both of you guys," Ron said, sitting down. "Well, not you." He pointed to Graig.

Tomás burst out again, laugh-crying until he coughed. Graig joined, the tears contagious. Ron called the server, motioning for something to drink, and writing with an invisible pen in the air. The tears and laughter and coming apart had subsided. The server came back with a pitcher of water. She set it down, along with the bill.

"You guys are having a ball over here," she said. "Or is this something else? A therapy session?"

"You could say that," Graig said.

"Thanks, hon," Ron said. "And what was your name?"

She pointed to her name tag. "Melanie," she said.

Tomás looked up her, and his face twisted up all over again.

Melanie frown-smiled, her eyebrows pitching upward.

"Oh, you poor thing," she said, touching Tomás's shoulder. "You boys take your time. I'll come back."

JOURNEY TO THE EDGE OF THE EARTH

Carl wiped his face and stopped laughing, his belly heaving to prepare for another set of sobs. He reached for a tissue, dabbed his eyes and blew his nose. He did this only in therapy: a visceral mixture of sadness and happiness, where he often doubled over, holding his solar plexus as though to gather in what was spilling out. Tony, his therapist, called it the intersection of sorrow and elation, and said it was a good thing to have those emotions come up like that. Carl had asked if this was perhaps mania and did he need to be on meds. Tony usually brushed this off, but said if he wanted a referral to psychiatry, he could do that for Carl.

"What's coming up for you right now?" Tony said.

"I'm just, I'm just torn, you know. I've got so much going for me. I have everything going for me, but—" Carl burst into laughter again.

"But what?" Tony said.

"It's all a lie."

"Talk about that a little bit more," Tony said.

"It's like I've said, I built this following—this platform, this, this—ideology—and they all believe me. They believe *in* me, but it's all just lies."

Tony said nothing.

"People send me hundreds of messages daily thanking me, praising me, telling me to stick it to science, and I should—like, this would be the moment, but it would all just fall apart. My whole argument. What scientist would debate a fucking quack?"

"Is that how you see yourself?" Tony said.

"Well, yes. And no. I mean, I have some evidence, and I stand by that, but I know it's not real. I mean, the earth is indeed round. You would have to be a fucking idiot to believe it was flat. And that's what I've done: I've stoked this idea for thousands, hundreds of thousands of people, and they eat it up."

"And that's what bothers you. That you know it's a lie, but you've persuaded others into believing it."

"Yes, I mean, that's what we're talking about here, right?" Carl said, always trying to decipher whether Tony's sentences were questions or statements.

"Yes, and that's what we call cognitive dissonance," Tony said. "You're fully aware that your thoughts and beliefs are inconsistent with your behavior. At one point, you believed what you were sharing, right? And then you didn't. When and why did that change?"

"I remember when I was really young, I saw this painting of a ship from the Age of Exploration going over the edge of the water. It fascinated me and sparked my curiosity. So, I started researching about the earth being flat, studying all the concepts. I found all these facts and information about it, then I discovered this group of flat earthers, and joined them. They loved that I was the youngest one."

Tony stayed silent.

"Fast forward, and then I started my TikTok page and then that was when everything skyrocketed. More people in the world became believers, and so I just sort of leaned into it. I gave them what they wanted."

Carl looked out the vertical blinds to the grassy courtyard. He had stopped laugh-crying. He looked back at Tony, who was waiting. Carl began to wring his hands. He breathed in, using some of the techniques they had worked on a long time ago in therapy, before he had any conflicts with his web of misinformation. Back then, therapy was a place to work through his issues with self-confidence and image, a way to process the anxiety and the occasional voice that crept in and told him that he was nothing, that he would amount to nothing. He and Tony had unearthed a deep family fossil, that originated with Carl's father conditioning him to feel bad about himself. He was over that now. *The past is past and set in stone and there is nothing I can do about it.*

"I mean, it just took over me, but then when I met Alexis, she poked holes in it. You know, just to be funny. I mean she loved me—she still loves me—but she sort of pushed me into the future somehow and told me it wouldn't last. That people would figure it out. That they would figure me out."

"Have they?"

"Well, not my followers. I mean, we're selling a god damn Journey to the Edge of the Earth tour for Christ's sake."

"We as in—?"

"Well, she's on board with all of it. She promotes all of this on her YouTube channel and everything. It's like she called out my bullshit, but then kind of doubled down on it. She pretty much co-opted it."

"And does she have similar sentiments? Does she have the cognitive dissonance that you feel?"

"I mean, I don't know. She doesn't seem to care."

"She doesn't care," Tony said. Not a question, not a statement.

"I mean, she doesn't have a problem with the fact that it's a lie and that I—that we—are making our livelihood out of it," Carl said.

"Okay."

Tony and his eternity-length pauses.

"What?" Carl said.

"What *what*?"

"Are you going to say something? Or ask me something?" Carl said.

"No. Do you want to say something? Something else about this?"

"Well, I mean—" Carl stared out the window again. "She doesn't have a problem with it, but I do, and now I'm kind of feeling like it's too much for me."

"Upholding what you've made," Tony said.

"Yes. I think I'm ready to call it quits. This whole platform. This whole idea."

"Okay."

"Okay, what?" Carl said.

"Nothing." Tony smiled. "I'm listening to you tell me what you want."

"Okay, now what?" Carl said.

"So, now what?" Tony said. "You just said what you want. So, what are you going to do about it?"

Carl breathed deep. He held his breath at the top, then exhaled.

"I think I need to tell her," he said.

"What are you going to tell her?"

"That it has to end. That she has to end it, too."

"How do you feel?" Tony said.

"Better," Carl said. "Clearer."

"Good," Tony said. "That's a good thing."

Carl stood in the front of his light ring, pressed record on his phone. He had to do it in this take because he was tired and wanted to take a nap.

"Hey, hey, fam, what's good? So, who's excited out there for the Journey? Can't wait! Look, I'll keep it short and sweet. Ship departs in eight days—EIGHT DAYS—from Long Beach. There's still time to register if you haven't already. We've got space for about ten more people, but we've passed the Early Bird registration, so DM me if you'd still like to take part and we can negotiate. But if you're already registered, no sweat, you're good! We'll meet at Café 301 for breakfast at 8 a.m. sharp on April 30, then shuttle to the port. Then we set sail. I emailed you the details. Hit me up with questions! Can't wait! Flat earth, mother fuckers!"

They had room for more. A lot more. So far, only four people had registered and paid the full fare. Carl and Alexis were lucky they could still charter the boat they wanted. The plan was to sail from Long Beach south to Isla Guadalupe, where they would dock for a night, then head out to the middle of the Pacific. They would qualify that they simply couldn't go much further to see the ice ring because that was where the current could sweep them over the edge. It would simply be too dangerous. The guests included an older couple from Fresno and a father and his young son coming in from Idaho. Carl and Alexis had figured, given the guests' ages and enthusiasm, that the pair could uphold their guests' gullibility with more stories and folklore and sumptuous meals.

Carl shut off his equipment and went to the bedroom. It was 9 a.m. He was usually off to the gym by then. Alexis had just finished her posts for the day. Her message on her channel, *Toxic Positivity*, that morning was an homage to a *Rick and Morty* episode where Jerry Smith had met a talking cat. The cat had challenged Jerry with the statement: "I think it's time you stopped asking questions and started having fun." Alexis had run with that, then closed with a plug for The Journey to the Edge of the Earth.

Carl, curled in the fetal position, draped a bandana over his eyes. Soon after, he felt Alexis curl in behind him.

"Babe? You okay?" she nibbled his ear.

"Just tired."

"Seems like you get really tired the days after your therapy. You want to talk?"

"No. I'm just going to take a nap."

"Well, I'm going to work, okay? Can I bring you something?"

He pulled the bandana off his face and turned to her.

"What?" she said.

"I don't know. I'm just. I'm worried about the trip."

"What about?"

"It's only a few people, and we'll probably have to pay more out of pocket. I mean, I think we're just going to break even."

"That's fine. Don't worry about. It'll be over, and then we won't have to do it again."

Carl exhaled.

"What?" Alexis sat up, looked at her watch.

"It's just—it's all such a fraud."

"Honey, we both know it. I know it. We've talked about it. It's just to help build the brand."

"But I think I'm done with it. I just—I don't want to keep doing this."

Alexis held his face, kissed him. She kissed his neck, than ran a hand up his shirt.

"We're going to be fine. You're going to be fine. You've worked too hard to give all this up."

He turned away from her.

"I have to go." She pulled her hand out of his shirt, then patted his rear. "Get up. Go to the gym. See you tonight."

He tried to sleep, but the nap wouldn't come. He lied there for a while trying some box breathing, then did what he normally did. He reached for his phone and opened TikTok. Over four-thousand views. Three-thousand, seven-hundred and two likes and counting. Fifteen new direct messages. Two more interested passengers.

I've always wanted to meet you, and I've decided to bite the bullet and join you guys! Just tell me how much. I don't care the amount. I'll pay it. Please let me know. I'll take out a loan or whatever I have to do. Can they accommodate a wheelchair?

@flatplanetpat

Hello Carl, your last post just got me thinking. Why not? This is a once in a lifetime opportunity. Can you let me know what the rate would be if I join now? I can get to Long Beach no problem. I live in Phoenix, so it's a relatively easy drive. Could I pay you in installments? Maybe half now, then half when I get my Social Security next month? I'm good for the money! Also, do you think we will need outer wear, such as parkas or beanies? If we're that close to the ice ring? Please advise.

Kind Regards,
Ralph McEvers, Jr.
Sun City, Arizona

Then the hate.

Hey fucknut: when will you wake up and smell the reality? Are you seriously going through with this? This is absolute buffoonery.

You know what, I hope you and the idiots on board your little cruise actually do fall off the face of the earth. Less of you on this planet would be a good thing.

17th Century much?

HORSESHIT!

Carl couldn't go on. Each one cut deeper than the last. He inhaled, tried to hold his breath as long as he could—he was up to a minute on good days—then let it all out in a cathartic gush. It was one of the few things he could do to get out of bed. He sat up, stretched, then managed to put on his gym clothes. He would respond to the interested passengers later, after he had pushed his body to exhaustion, after he'd filled himself with protein, cold-showered, and summoned up his character, the pseudo-scientist known as Carl "Flat Manly" Bonifacio.

Alexis returned from work carrying bags from Wood Ranch. Carl's favorite.

He stood to help her. He'd been on the couch most of the afternoon, tired, not energized after his workout.

"Oh my gosh, Wood Ranch. What's the occasion?" he said.

She was smiling, eyes bright and expectant.

"I've got good news," she said.

"What is it?" He felt a real smile on his face.

"Let's eat first."

"Nah, just tell me."

She set the food on the table, grabbed his hands.

"Eeek, get ready!"

"What, what is it? I'm dying here," he said.

"Joe Rogan wants you on his podcast!"

"What? Joe Rogan? Like *the* Joe Rogan?"

"The Joe Rogan!" Alexis shook Carl's arms up and down, pulled him in for a hug.

"Wow! How? What are the details?"

"Well, this guy named Steve, he's part of Rogan's production company, DM'd me. He said he's been trying to contact you. Are you checking your DM's? Anyway, he said he tried to reach out because they heard about the cruise and they want to know more. He said they're going to have some other flat earthers on, too."

That air Carl had breathed in and let out earlier, seemed to escape him now in totality. There was no way he could do this. Rogan, though an idol of his, would see right through it. He'd give him the space to debate, but it wouldn't end well. Plus, with other flat earthers there, it would be disastrous. If there was anyone that Carl did not directly associate with, it was other flat earth experts. He'd learned early on that the leaders in the ideology were notoriously insufferable. Together, they were more like dysfunctional siblings upholding their own versions of a family façade that did very little to strengthen their cause.

"You're not excited about this." Alexis dropped his hands.

"Um. Well, I don't know. I think I am. I need to give this some thought." He took at seat at the dining table.

"It's Joe Rogan," Alexis said. "You'll skyrocket."

"Yeah, but maybe not in a good way."

"Look, maybe just take the opportunity, then see what happens." She sat, placed her hand on his.

Carl stared off, like he did when in Tony's office. He tapped into what he learned most recently in therapy. That he has to state what he wants, that he needs to ask for what he needs, when he needs it.

"What changed for you" he said, "with all this stuff? When did you believe in it, too?"

"You're still thinking about ending all of this, right?"

"You didn't answer my question," he said.

"It was that," she said. "That you were always so curious and questioning. It was early on, I think when I started following you, that I thought, 'Okay, this guy is ridiculous, but he's actually making me question if the world is actually a globe, and that's a good thing. He's challenging me to think differently.' That's what I thought was cool about it. About you. That you simply made people question reality."

"But then you—made it yours, too," Carl said.

"I did. I admit that. But I did because I love you and I support you."

"Not because you're trying to build a brand, too?"

Alexis looked down, then back up at him.

"We're a couple. We're supposed to support each other, right?"

"I love you," he said. "You're my everything."

"Why does it feel like something bad is coming?"

"It's not bad. It's just change."

"What do you mean? Where is this going?"

"I'm quitting this. I'm cancelling the trip, I'm giving those people their money back. It's over. I'm—I'm just done."

"But you can't—you're Flat Manly. You're—"

"No, I'm not. I don't want to be that anymore. And I just need your support. I'm going to fall, obviously, but it has to happen. I have to be something else. Be someone else. It's time."

"I'm just, so confused. I thought it was like something you could do, like a character, then put away. I mean, isn't that what we're doing here? It's like my channel. I don't believe all that stuff either. It's just what I say to people."

"To people who believe in you," he said.

"People believe in you, too."

"And now I want them to know the truth. My truth."

Alexis inhaled, her chin quivered, her eyes brimming with tears.

"Okay. I get it. I mean, I know it's going to hurt, but if this is what you want."

"It is what I want. It's what I need."

"What about this Joe Rogan thing?" she said, wiping her yes.

"I want to do it. I want to get this off my chest," Carl said.

Sitting on the sofa across from Tony, Carl spread his arms out, draping them over the back of the couch.

"You seem much more relaxed," Tony said. "Your whole demeanor reflects calm."

"Thank you. I feel it. I told my girlfriend what I wanted, and she accepted it," Carl said.

"What was her reaction?"

"She was sad. She cried."

"It's kind of like how you cried in our last session. Perhaps you two are mourning the change that's coming," Tony said.

"That sounds about right," Carl said.

"So, what's next?"

"I'm telling my followers. I'm cancelling this trip. Oh, and I'm going to go on the Joe Rogan Experience and debunk it all."

"Wow! The Joe Rogan Experience?" Tony said.

"Do you listen to it?"

"No, but I hear it has quite a following."

"Yeah, it's going to be big," Carl said.

"What's going to be big?" Tony said. "The show?"

"No, the announcement. Once I say what I'm going to say on his show, it's going to get some attention."

"And what are you going to say?"

Carl pulled his arms off the back of the couch and leaned forward, palms up outstretched to Tony.

"That the world is round. Of course."

"And you're expecting to feel attention?"

Carl sat back.

"Well—yeah."

"May I ask you something?" Tony said.

"Yeah. What?"

"My job isn't to judge you. My job is to provide a space for you to talk and share your feelings. A place for you to process your emotions. And so, I don't want this question to come across as judgmental. Maybe just more a curiosity."

Carl pulled his arms in, holding his elbows in a half self-hug. Tony went on.

"I'm not one who believes that the earth is flat. I like to consider myself a man of science, and the scientific tradition I ascribe to tells me that the earth is indeed round. But, I also believe people should and are able to believe what they want to believe, right? So, when I first met you and you shared that you believed the earth was flat, I didn't judge, but I did question that belief. I wondered how you arrived at that and why you upheld that. It all came clear to me later, once you shared what you did and all that, but I still just kind of wondered about what drove you to be so adamant about that notion. I had kind of forgotten about it until just now, when you said you were expecting to feel attention."

"This is the longest way to ask a question, Tony," Carl said. "I'm dying here."

"First of all, never say your dying, okay? The brain only hears what it hears and the body responds. And yes, here's the question. Forgive the preamble. When you began building your platform, gaining followers, becoming Flat Manly, were you doing it because you wanted to make a real change in the world—in other words, did you want to change hearts and minds, or were you simply wanting to feel something, like attention?"

Carl had no words. He now steeped his hands together, prayer like, his fingertips at his lips. His eyes searched, first the neutral carpet of Tony's office, then the coffee table and tissue box, the bookshelves filled with psychology manuals, then the modern art, and then his own thoughts. It was attention.

"Wow, Tony. Wow."

"Again, I'm not trying to judge you here. And I don't think it's incredibly relevant to your mental state right now, I just—"

"No, it's not judgmental. But I do think it's relevant. I mean, I just wanted to feel something, and I went about it seeking attention."

"Well, just spend some more time thinking about that. Maybe you can identify the moment when it went from a true interest to filling some unmet need. But right now, I invite you to hold onto the distinctions you've made so far."

"No, no, you don't have to do all the psychology talk. I get it, I get it. It's just making mesee it now in full. I've felt what I needed to feel, and now I feel something different. Thank you for helping me see that."

Carl sat back again, exhaled.

"And I know what you're going to say," he said.

"And what's that?" Tony said.

"What's next?"

With that, Tony crossed his legs, and clasped his own hands together.

Hello @flatplanetpat

I'm writing to let you know that the Journey to the Edge of the Earth has been cancelled. Soon, I will be providing more details about this change in plans, as well as change in my stance on this theory that unites us. For the moment, know that there is nothing you need to do since you have not paid. I simply ask for your patience and understanding as I sort out what comes next. I sincerely thank you for your interest and support of me and my platform. You mentioned a wheelchair. I'm curious to know more about your condition, and I'm wondering how I might support your health journey.

Sincerely,
Carl "Flat Manly" Bonifacio

Dear Mr. McEvers,

First, I would like to thank you for making direct contact with me to state your interest in the Journey to the Edge of the Earth. It's fans like you that inspire me to do what I do. Second, I must inform you that the voyage has been cancelled due to a significant change in how I view Planet Earth. I hope that what I am about to share does not erode your own beliefs, nor take away the awe and mystery of science and the wonder of what we cannot see nor explain, I hope that you are able to stay curious about Earth and space and science, and that you find your own way to explain your theories and belief systems, and that you hold true to them for however long they work for you.

For me, I have arrived at a new understanding that the earth is not flat, and that it is indeed round. I once believed that it was flat and found theories to support it, but there is overwhelming evidence that Earth is round, and over time, I have not been able to ignore it, nor have I been able to continue upholding what I know is simply false. Processing this change, going from someone who was a true believer, someone who was a prominent voice in the Flat Earth community, to someone who is now denouncing the entire belief system and calling it a hoax, has been a journey in and of itself. I hope that this does not shake you in a harmful way. I am trying to be honest with the community, which will most certainly include me stepping away from it.

As mentioned, please stay curious. Embrace the mystery of it all. Question everything and believe when you're ready.

Sincerely,
Carl Bonifacio

To: *The Joe Rogan Experience*

From: *Carl Bonifacio*

Hello Steve and Team,

First, thank you so much for your interest in my message, and for considering me to be a guest on the show. When my girlfriend shared the news about your offer, I was thrilled. But, I admit I was also incredibly afraid. I'll explain. At the time of your offer, I was in the middle of a major shift in my identity. I have since rejected that notion that the earth is flat, and I am dismantling my platform, which upholds this belief, if you want to call it that. Because of my fame and notoriety in this field, there is a lot of work to be done to reframe my position. There was a moment when I wanted to join your show to become a vocal opponent of flat earthers, but I checked myself, asking, "What will this serve other than adding more noise to a ludicrous topic in the first place?"

And so, with all due respect, I decline your request to be a guest on your show. I'm sure it's going to be a lively discussion that will accomplish very little for those involved.

Sincerely,

Carl Bonifacio

Formerly known as Flat Manly

HERCULES MARTINEZ

The faint odor of sweating bodies hit Blas's nose once inside the train leaving Waterloo station. He was surprised—as developed as England was, there was very little air conditioning. But no matter. Where he'd just come from, there was no forced air either. Yet, there, in San Jose del Pacifico, the heat was negligible. He had adapted to the fresh air of the Oaxaca highlands, and he'd forgotten about the extremes in temperature in cities as large as London.

Blas had never been to London, and immediately he felt out of place. Most of the people—at least on this train—were pale and pasty. The women reminded him of all his exes: fair-haired maidens of Scandinavian descent, long necked and still holding onto their ancestors' cool demeanors. Living in Oaxaca the last six months he'd had an epiphany that reaffirmed what his uncles and cousins had been chiding him about since puberty—"Better to date within your gene pool, unless, of course, you're intentionally trying to improve la raza." Followed by, "...but that's never a bad thing."

Blas accused them of having a colonizer mindset, and confirmed he simply preferred blondes. But that all went away in Mexico. While finding his calling, Blas had dated a couple of women, who, in previous worlds would have never been his type, yet there was a built-in cultural awareness, and, though he hated to admit it, there was some playing out of traditional gender roles he'd never experienced with his Caucasian girlfriends. Never before had dinner been waiting for him, or his laundry folded. He had always been the gardener, never the garden.

"Now arriving, Wandsworth," the soothing British woman's voice said. "Wandsworth," she said again, the train easing to a halt.

Blas stepped out, minding the gap as he'd been told, it seemed, at every turn since arriving in England. Once down the stairs, he encountered a street filled with coffee shops and small restaurants, diners at tables spilling onto the avenue, which itself was closed to traffic.

Que bonita, he thought. He loved that he was still thinking in Spanish.

This was nothing like the cobbled road leading into and out of San Jose del Pacifico. No vendors selling serapes or carved pipes or those mysterious shaman-like folks that emerged out of nowhere asking if he wanted to buy any hongos. Blas never bought his hongos. He only received them from his maestro, don Luis Martinez, and that was only after four months there. Don Luis told him he would know when he was ready to receive the mushroom, which don Luis called, "his son."

Stashed in his backpack, wrapped snug in tinfoil, and nestled into his water bottle, Blas had transported two of don Luis's children—with his permission—all the way to England.

"Will they still have their power?" Blas asked his maestro.

"Ja, ja, ja," don Luis laughed. "Crees que hice un debilucho? No. Pero, das prisa," don Luis advised. "Les da aire y sol lo mas pronto posible. Y cuando ustedes están listos, empieze la ceremonia."

When you and your friend are ready, begin the ceremony…

Blas knew it wasn't going to be that easy. He'd need a day or two or three to adjust to the time change, and he'd have to prepare Eduardo physically, mentally, and spiritually. And, he'd want to make sure Eduardo's meds had washed out. He could not do the ceremony under the influence of those pills. It just wouldn't be the same. They would go exercise, preferably at a gym, where they could push and pull and grunt and scream if needed to release negative energies. Or they could go for a run, but Eduardo wasn't much of a runner. Or they could do a lot of yoga. And eat healthy and drink tea, and pray, and write their intentions. God, how long had it been, really, since they saw each other?

The wedding. Holy shit. The wedding.

Blas knew that. He'd just kind of blocked it out. Time had marched on since last summer. Blas thought, it's not every day you go from being someone's best man to their personal spiritual healer, followed by, fuck, it's hot.

After the cute street, the neighborhood turned average. Not that Blas was expecting much. He was in the suburbs now. No Big Ben, no Tower of London. But he wasn't here to sightsee. He was here to heal. To cure. No, not to cure. No one cures anyone of anything. Only guides them toward healing. But, damn, if anyone needed to be cured, it was Eduardo. Poor guy. Eight months into his marriage and he found out Stella had been seeing her ex. Sent Eduardo into a downward spiral. He was already anxious as it was. Had to adjust his meds a few times. That's what all this was for. To atone for Blas not being there—at least in person—when Eduardo was at his worst. They talked every day. Blas encouraged him to pick up and move to the UK like he'd always wanted. Get out of New Mexico. And Eduardo said he loved the idea of Blas moving to Oaxaca to finally follow his path to be a curandero.

Blas's phone buzzed, his Siri, a Mexican woman, telling him when to turn. He'd arrived. Queen Adelaide. Eduardo's local pub. Their most recent WhatsApp exchanges felt more real, closer.

Eduardo: We're going straight to lunch after your red eye. You CANNOT go to sleep!
Blas: Right arm
Eduardo: Lol I'm going to take you to a proper English pub
Blas: Proper! Como qué proper???
Eduardo: No drinking that day. It'll kill you. But we will go out the next night (beers emoji)
Blas: Right on (flexed arm emoji)

Blas hadn't quite told Eduardo that he'd quit drinking alcohol, and he was prepared to illuminate Eduardo on the dangers of it, that it will indeed kill you.

Sandals shuffling over the tiled entry, Blas found the pub quiet and empty. He peered around.

"Can I help you, mate?" The bartender said.

"I'm looking for my friend."

"You're the only one here," The bartender said. "Grab a seat and we'll let you know when he arrives. Can I get you something?"

"Iced tea, please."

"Did you say iced tea?" The bartender tried to hold in a laugh.

"Yeah, just landed."

"Right. Go on and I'll bring it over."

Blas sat near a window and dropped his bag. He thought he might see Eduardo coming up. He ran his hands through his long hair and scratched his beard. He breathed in and thought this is probably just the kind of country Eduardo needs. Quiet. Polite.

Boring. He wondered if he might still be on the same dose of antidepressants. This place might require more.

The tea arrived.

"Thank you," Blas said.

"Is there anything else we can get you while you wait?"

Blas scanned the menu placard, "I'll just wai—" and he looked up. Eduardo stood over him holding a tray, grinning at Blas.

"You mother fucker!" Blas sprung to his feet. "Get over here!"

The best friend hug. Almost a year overdue.

"You look good, mate! The beard. The hair!" Eduardo said.

"Wait, wait, wait, what is this accent?" Blas laughed. "*Mate?...*phh."

"Oh shush, I live in bloody England!" Eduardo said.

"Shut the fuck up, homie, you're from Taos, New Mexico." Blas said. *Was this an—act?*

"Come on then, tea time." Eduardo said, motioning them to sit.

"Dude, no seriously, what the fuck's up with your voice?" Blas said.

"Comes and goes," Eduardo said.

The bartender came over. "It worked!" he said. "You must be Blas." The bartender extended a hand. "Nick."

"You were in on this?" Blas laughed.

"Of course," Nick said. "We love Eddie. The usual?" Nick smacked Eduardo on the back.

"Yeah, mate," Eduardo said.

"I'll bring one for Blas. Oh, and he explained your name. You two are kind of like Spaniards, but not really. More like natives, right? But anyway, I get the blahs, too, sometimes. This weather here will do it to you." Nick pointed and winked at Eduardo.

"Fucking guy," Eduardo said.

"Wow, you're like a local," Blas said.

"Yeah, I've been—assimilating," Eduardo said.

"I can tell. I mean, you look great too. You been working out?"

"Walking. That's all I do here. I love it."

"Okay, there's your voice," Blas said. "I was beginning to worry."

Nick returned with two pints of beer. "Enjoy, gents. Catch up."

"I thought you said no beer on day one," Blas said.

"Ah, it won't kill you. Come on. It's been too long. Salud."

Blas toasted with his tea, pushed the pint of beer aside.

They drank, smiled, and fell into a familiar rhythm, though the music was different. The lyrics had changed. The harmony wasn't quite right. Yet. It was like their former lives when Blas was on bass and Eduardo was on guitar. It always took them a little time to find each other in the music.

"But seriously, how are you? Blas sipped his tea.

"I'm good," Eduardo said. "I'm much better than I was."

"Man, I wanted to come out to see you sooner, but you know, it's been a busy time."

"No, I get it. It's been good for me to be alone and get my head right. It helps to be somewhere foreign because you have to relearn everything. Well shit, same for you. Tell me about Mexico. And like, you're a shaman now!"

"Curandero," Blas said. And not officially. I don't have a card or anything. It's something you work on your whole life. I'm just at the beginning."

"I'm happy for you. You've always wanted to do this. You're making it happen," Eduardo swigged a large gulp.

"It feels really good," Blas said. He glanced at Eduardo's pint, which was nearing the halfway point.

"But, like you feel good though?" Blas went on. "Are you having any symptoms or anything?"

Eduardo crunched his brow. "No, what do you mean?"

"I mean, is there a part of your body that hurts, or is it mostly in your head?"

"Is what mostly in my head?" Eduardo drank, licked his lips, pushed back. "This feels weird all of a sudden. Are you doing some spell on me or something?" He laughed.

"No, it's not like that," Blas said. "I don't do spells. Come on, I'm just curious about you. I want to help you."

"So what, you don't drink?" Eduardo said.

"Well, no. I stopped. It's really bad for you. It's poisonous," Blas said.

"Well, shit, these next two weeks are going to be boring," Eduardo said.

"We don't need to drink to have fun. We're going to have fun, man."

"Yeah. Let's uh, finish up here, and I'll show you the place. It's just down the way," Eduardo said.

"There's that accent again!" Blas laughed, reaching over the table to grab Eduardo's shoulder.

Eduardo returned a smile and the slightest wink of his right eye. That was a new thing too, the wink.

Eduardo's place was five flights up in a white modern building with lots of windows. It blended into what seemed like a village of unremarkable high rises. They took the stairs.

"I've learned to avoid the elevator," Eduardo said. "This is my daily workout. Two steps at a time. Oh, there's coffee right there." He pointed from the third-floor landing where the tall window gave a view into an inner courtyard amongst a few other buildings. "You still drink coffee, right?" Eduardo laughed.

"Yes, yes. And I love that you're taking the stairs. It's so good for you. Any kind of movement is good for you," Blas said. "It's natural medicine."

Eduardo unlocked the door to unit 504 and opened it wide for Blas. "Here we are."

"Wow. It's so…clean." The word Blas wanted to say was empty. Eduardo was famous for hoarding. All his previous places were filled with books, magazines, piles of papers, receipts, electronics, gadgets, all of it.

"Yeah, thanks," Eduardo said. "That's one good thing I picked up from Stella—organizational skills. And from my therapist. He helped me to let go of attachments. Still learning that one."

"I'm very proud of you," Blas said, pulling his friend in for another hug.

"Thanks. Follow me." Eduardo led Blas down a small hallway. "Bathroom." He pointed. "And your room. It's not much. It's like Harry Potter's cupboard under the stairs."

Across from the bathroom was a narrow side room meant for an office or storage nook. It had a small high window and the floor was covered with cushions and pillows. Under the window on the small table sat a Buddha and some candles.

"It's perfect," Blas said. "Is this—

"It's my meditation room," Eduardo said. "My thinking room. I come here to relax, chill out. I knew you'd like it."

Blas set his bag down. All of this was—not quite overwhelming nor shocking, but more unexpected. Eduardo was…someone else now.

"My room's upstairs. The loft. Wanna see?" Eduardo said.

"Dude, I can't believe I'm going to say this, but I think I need to lie down."

"Yeah, this room can suck you in. But don't sleep, like I said. It will mess you up."

"No, I think I really do need to sleep. I'm kinda dizzy," Blas said. And he was. The exhaustion, the emotions, they smacked him hard.

"Okay, okay. Only a short nap, but I'm going to come wake you up. We're going to dinner tonight."

"I'll be fine," Blas said. "I need to listen to my body."

"Okay, you do that." Eduardo smiled. "You really are a healer now. Listen to your body."

Blas hit the cushions and was out. He sunk in and was soon dreaming of San Jose del Pacifico. He was with don Luis, and they were sitting side by side atop a bluff in the mountains where a space in the trees showed the misty valley below. They went there in the mornings to watch the sun rise. Don Luis said he must face east and ask the spirit every morning to guide him. He said once a day, the spirit comes in some form meant just for you. Pay attention to that, he said. Listen to it. Observe it. Receive it. In his dream, Blas turned toward don Luis and don Luis turned to him, but instead of his face, it was Eduardo, smiling and winking.

Blas came to and sat up, blinking his eyes awake in disbelief. He looked up at the window: a faint light, not quite bright enough to make him squint, poured in. He stood to stretch but still felt heavy with exhaustion. On the table next to Buddha was a note and his phone, plugged into the wall.

The note read:

Good morning! I couldn't wake you. Ha ha!
I bet you 10 pounds it'll be about 4 am when you get this. Go back to sleep!
I wake up at about 7. We'll get coffee. I plugged your phone in.
Told you not to take a nap, carnal!!!

Blas tapped his phone. 4:15 a.m.

There was no going back to sleep now. He was refreshed. Disoriented, but rested. Plus, he remembered the children. They needed sun and air as don Luis instructed. He dug into his carry-on bag, found the water bottle. It had been almost 24 hours. Oaxaca to Mexico City, Mexico City to Miami, Miami to London, followed by his ten hour nap. He prayed they were still there, still viable, and fresh. Don Luis said you would know by the smell. Did they still have some of the dust on the surface? If so, they would be fine. And they don't need that much time in the sun. Afterward, put them back in a container. Keep them dry. Cool.

He unwrapped the tinfoil. They still smelled as potent as the moment Don Luis set them in Blas's hand. Of course they would be just as strong. This was Hercules Martinez. Not quite a god, not quite a man.

Blas found a small plate in the kitchen and set the two mushrooms on it. He opened a sliding door just off the tiny living and dining area. The space was not a balcony, and also not *not* a balcony. A place for half of your body to get some air. To hang a few clothes. To smoke. The sun was rising, and not from dense fog across a high desert landscape, but from behind a brutal building shaped like a rising triangle. Blas set the plate on the ledge, minding the potential fall. He waited for the sun to peek out and pour its rays on him and the children. He closed his eyes and asked the spirit his daily request.

Espíritu, gracias por todas las bendiciones que me has dado. Por favor, guíame para ser la mejor versión de mí mismo

Spirit, thank you for all you have blessed me with. Please guide me to be the best version of myself.

"Are you praying?" Eduardo's voice snapped Blas out of his morning moment.

"Whoa, what are you doing up?" Blas said.

"I knew you'd be awake. And, I couldn't sleep."

"Why not? Something on your mind?" Blas said.

"No, I just couldn't sleep, you know. Excited you're here. Wait, are those…?" Eduardo pointed to the small plate.

Blas beamed with pride. "Yep, these are the children."

"Hercules?" Eduardo asked.

"Yes, Hercules Martinez. Grown by my maestro, Luis Martinez. It's a new strain."

Eduardo made his signature tiny whistle through pursed lips. Blas knew this meant doubt.

It was his friend's way of saying something without saying it. He used to do it all the time back in the day.

"Cool, huh?" Blas said. "They're good."

"How many times you done them?" Eduardo said.

"Well, you don't really do this kind of medicine." Blas brought the plate back inside and went to the kitchen, opening cabinets. "You practice them."

"Here," Eduardo stepped in. "What are you looking for?"

"A little container to store these," Blas said. "Only once."

"What?" Eduardo opened a lower drawer and fished out a small Tupperware. "Here."

"I've only eaten them once," Eduardo said.

"Oh. Huh. Once was enough, I guess?" Eduardo rubbed his face. "Well, do you want to go practice some coffee?"

"Isn't it a bit early? And no, once was just the beginning. You learn something new each time…Now, it's time to share them."

"There's a shop that opens at 5. It's close to the river," Eduardo said. "I'm going to throw some clothes on."

"Okay." Blas opened the fridge. Mostly empty but except for spinach, eggs, and, to his surprise, mushrooms.

At Cat's Paw, they stood waiting, already a small line at about 5:30 a.m.

"So, you still black and sugar?" Blas said. Eduardo ignored his question as they moved forward in line.

Eduardo smiled at the barista. "Morning, love," he said, his accent back. "Cappuccino."

"Yak milk, right?" She said.

"My fave!" Eduardo chirped back.

"Yak?" Blas said.

"What can I get you?" The barista turned to Blas.

"Um, latte. What kind of milk do you have?"

"All but yak," she said.

"Oh, I get it," Blas said. "Soy, please."

"I got you, mate." Eduardo pulled out a card.

"There's that accent again," Blas said.

They sat outdoors. Blas studied his friend a bit. Maybe it was the jet lag, maybe the months that had turned into a year. Whatever, a dark thought crossed his mind: Eduardo had gotten worse. Maybe now he had a split personality. Maybe he was delusional. Maybe he was going crazy. There was that one time they did acid after a show when all Eduardo wanted to do was go out in the backyard and hide in the shed. Blas and the band had to pull him back inside the house and turn on the Smurfs and feed him some Captain Crunch to bring him back to reality.

"What?" Eduardo said. "You're oddly quiet."

"I don't know. It's been a long time." Blas learned forward. "And, I'm kinda worried about you. You've got this accent, and you're all chipper and shit. Are you on different meds now?"

Eduardo pulled his lips tight, shook his head, seemed to be gathering his thoughts.

"You know, my therapist has taught me something really important, and that's having boundaries. I don't have to share anything I don't want to," Eduardo said.

"Dude, what? I'm your best friend," Blas said. "And I'm not trying to force you or anything. I'm just asking if you're okay."

"Well, suddenly you're some kind of healer and all you want to do is check in on me like you're a doctor or something. I'm fine."

"Look, I don't know what's going on. I'm just here to help. We're obviously not—we're just out of sync or something," Blas said.

"Yeah, I wanted to tell you…I don't know how to say this…I don't think I need your help," Eduardo said.

Blas sat back. He'd brought everything. His sahumerio, his copal, his red bandana. Teas, herbs. Hercules Martinez. They had chatted about this on WhatsApp over the past few months. What was he going to do now?

"I came all this way," Blas said.

"Because you wanted a patient, or what?" Eduardo said.

"It's not how it works," Blas said. "I'm just going to go back to your house," he said, "I'm pretty tired." He stood, started walking.

"It's that way," Eduardo pointed in the opposite direction, tossed him the keys.

"See ya." Blas caught them and headed back into the sea of white buildings.

Blas wasn't too deep into his morning nap in the mediation room, when he felt a presence, a body—Eduardo—easing himself behind Blas, Eduardo gently draping his arm over his friend.

"Hey," Blas exhaled, fluttered his eyes open. "Thanks."

"Remember this?" Eduardo said.

"Yeah. When the last time?"

"Oh, god, I don't know. The bachelor party?"

Blas laughed. "Yeah. They always told us to get a room."

"We always ended up in bed together," Eduardo laughed.

"Maybe this is what we needed, huh?" Blas said. "Just our little cuddle time."

"Yeah, probably so," Eduardo said.

Their first time was out of necessity. They'd played at the Red River Brewery Winterfest and Beaner and Rodney wanted to get back to Taos before the snow. Eduardo and Blas were getting drunk and chiding the guys, telling them there was nothing to worry about, that the storm would pass and that they'd leave after some pizza. Beaner and Rodney left. The storm blew in with a vengeance, and the Department of Transportation closed the roads. Either way, Eduardo's Geo Metro would never make it through the mountain passes.

All the rooms in town were booked. Blas had charm-begged the Sky High Pies shop lady.

"I swear," he said, "we just need a warm place to sleep. We'll be out in the morning. We just played in the show. We're like rock stars, you know. Very unprepared rock stars."

Blas was the sweet talker, always getting them out of jams. She laughed, and then let them stay. She said they could sleep on the benches in the waiting area of the shop. She didn't tell them that once the pizza oven cooled, the place would drop into the 50s. No need to heat the restaurant from 10 pm to 10 am. Blas and Eduardo couldn't get comfortable on the benches. They found some sacks of flour in the walk-in pantry to use as makeshift pillows.

"I'm so fucking cold," Eduardo said.

They were parallel, their backs against the shelves filled with tomato sauce, olives, and mushrooms, just a few feet between them on the floor. Eduardo was also having a bad day. He'd botched his guitar solo on a cover of "Where Is My Mind," and the rest of the night went downhill from there. After the show, he cried and then the guys put a bottle of tequila in front of him, which they knew only worked as a Band-Aid.

"Well…uh…here, just…come over here," Blas said, always the problem solver. "Let's spoon or whatever. Body heat, you know?"

"No," Eduardo said. He started whimpering. Making pucheros. That bottom lip quivering with sadness.

"Well, you're the one that's cold," Blas said. "And I know you had a bad show."

"Fuck you," Eduardo said. "You're not cold?" He was now crying.

"Fuck yeah I'm cold." Blas shivered. They were really only in their black t-shirts and black jeans, let alone having no body fat in those days. Their parkas were now paltry blankets.

"Okay, whatever." Eduardo pushed his sack of flour to the middle of the room. Blas did the same. They wiggled closer, awkward and clinical at first, and then…connection. They fit like two puzzle pieces, Blas, the one in back.

"You gonna sing me a lullaby?" Eduardo laughed-cried, still drunk, still processing.

"Shut up," Blas said. "Go to sleep." He draped his arm over his friend as though it was nothing, and Eduardo, as though it was nothing, took that arm and hugged it. They slept warm and solid, and the next morning, they were in a reverse position, Blas in Eduardo's embrace.

Now, in Eduardo's meditation room, it felt like the old days. Whether it was that first time, or after a show in some small town—when they were actually making a name for themselves in the Southwest—or after a night of partying, and, if they hadn't taken a lady fan or the occasional groupie to bed, they found each other's embrace and went to sleep. Never any clothes off, never any touching nor kissing nor sex. They'd never even brought the subject up. It just felt like something they were supposed to do.

"Remember when the guys wanted to change the name of the band to Bromance?" Blas laughed.

"Those fucking guys. And all that time it was Rodney that was the gay one," Eduardo said.

"Do you think Rodney and Beaner ever…?" Blas said

"Nah. Beaner's not into guys," Eduardo said "Anyway, look, I'm not going to apologize for anything because I don't think I need to, but I could tell you're hurt. Or confused or something. I'm fine, man. Seriously. I'm not losing my mind or anything."

"Okay, I hear you. I just—yeah. I don't know. It's weird now. We're all grown up."

"Yeah, and we just have to accept that," Eduardo said.

"So, you're violating my boundaries right now," Blas smiled. "This spooning and all. You didn't ask."

"Stop. I know, I know. I must sound like a therapist. But, you sound like some witch doctor."

"First, it's not witchcraft." Blas looked back over his shoulder at Eduardo. "Second, I can help you."

"Okay, I'll let you. We'll do it. We'll do Hercules," Eduardo said.

"Right arm," Blas laughed.

"This one?" Eduardo said and draped his arm over Blas.

"Yeah," Blas said, snuggling back in.

"One more nap for old times." Eduardo said, and the two fell asleep.

The next several days, Eduardo complied with Blas's regimens. No drinking. No pub food. They kept up with the walking and saw some sights. They went to a gym and lifted weights. Blas led some yoga. They spooned every few nights, and most often it was only to fall asleep and then wake up on opposite sides of the mattress. They joked that as grown men, they were just too fat, sweaty, and hairy now to keep that up.

"We're almost ready for the ceremony," Blas said one day over lunch.

"What's left to do? Eduardo said.

"I have to ask about your medicine. I know you've always been on something, and I've never judged your journey, but I believe it would be best to be completely off whatever you're taking, at least a day or two before we do this."

The Eduardo pursed-lip whistle. The neither here nor there. The definitely maybe.

"What?" Blas said. "Do you think you can?"

"Well, I think the question is, should I?" Eduardo said.

"Have you missed any? Would a day or two set you back?"

"I don't know. I think I'll have to call my doctor," Eduardo said.

"No, no, no, don't do that. I would just—experiment."

"I don't know. I'm on a daily antidepressant plus the Zac for when I'm feeling a little extra anxious. I mean, I guess I could stop that. And if the journey is good, like, if I'm in a happy mood, I might not need to be on an antidepressant that day," Blas said.

"See, that's what I mean. We're talking about healing ourselves. We're our own healers. That's the first thing about being a healer."

"The first rule of fight club?" Eduardo said.

"Look, you are doing great. You've got this killer sense of humor now, your place is spotless. I think you're doing really amazing. After all you've been through?"

"Yeah, plus the talk therapy."

"Yes, and talk therapy," Blas said. "You're doing so well."

"But it took me a long time to get here, you know. It's not like I'm flirting with the barista because it comes naturally. I really have to work on all of this."

"Bro, I'm here for you, and if you don't want to do this, I totally get it. And I'm not doing my charming sales pitch thing or whatever you call it. I get it."

"I'm going to sleep on it. And I might ask my doc. Not my psychiatrist. My psychologist."

"Do what you gotta do. Sleep, talk. I'm here. Hercules Martinez is here. But I will say, not for long. Remember, I fly back next week. And if we just chill for the next five days, that's cool, too, okay?"

They chose the Wandsworth Common by Eduardo's building, which, on the weekends, was a cricket oval. There was a playground in the same field if they wanted to get goofy and a walking trail around the entire common so they could keep moving. And, the river was right there so they could see something different. They would also be close to the apartment if, worst case, they needed to go back and turn on the TV or go to sleep.

Blas instructed them to write their intentions down. Write down something you want to be free of, and something you want to receive.

"We have to let go of something in order to make space for the new," he said. "We'll take these with us to the park," he'd said.

Eduardo said he hadn't needed to take Prozac since Blas had arrived, so he wasn't worried there. He had stopped taking, two days prior, his antidepressant. He had no problems for a day, but the second day, the day leading into the night of their journey, he had trouble getting out of bed. Blas feared it might turn into the very old days, when Eduardo would sleep until 11, sometimes noon. He'd mope around until he had his coffee, then fall into some news infotainment before he went to work.

But not today, Blas pulled him out of bed. "Come on buddy, we're going to the gym."

They had a small breakfast and kept it light on the weights. Blas played feel good music all afternoon at the apartment. He knew the window was closing.

It was time. There, on a blanket they had spread out under a tall tree, the sun just set, Blas transferred the children from the plastic container to a ceremonial red cloth. Blas himself wore a white traditional guayabera with colorful trim on the sleeves and collar. He'd wrapped a red bandana around his forehead along with a woven sash around his waist. He adorned his wrists with leather bracelets and beads.

"You are so into this," Eduardo said, slapping Blas on the arm. "I love it."

"And I love you, bro. Are you ready?"

Eduardo exhaled. "Yeah, I'm ready." He put his hand out.

"Not so fast." Blas knelt down and lit a small piece of charcoal that was inside the chalice, and blew on it until it was glowing red. He placed a chunk of what looked like a white rock on top of it.

"The mighty copal," he said.

A bitter but fragrant smoke—piney and reminiscent of frankincense—wafted from the chalice. Blas blew on it making the smoke thicker. He took the chalice and walked it around Eduardo, blowing the smoke onto him.

"Receive the blessing," Blas said.

Eduardo coughed a bit, then Blas demonstrated with one hand how to pull the smoke toward himself and wash it over his body. Blas knelt down to Eduardo's feet, sending smoke all around him, and then set the chalice onto the smaller woven rug he had brought from Mexico.

"Now, we can either share our intentions for this journey with each other, or remain in silence," Blas said.

"Silence," Eduardo quickly said.

"That's…that's good," Blas said. He reached down to his smaller ceremonial rug and picked up the children. He placed one in Eduardo's palm.

"So, we just eat it, right?"

Blas nodded, serene and tranquil, placing his mushroom into his own mouth. He began chewing.

"Now, wait?" Eduardo said.

"Shhhh…" Blas knelt and began picking up his supplies. He let the copal burn and worked slow and deliberate, rolling up his blankets and placing his things in a small backpack.

"Let's walk," he said.

They began a lap around the park. Eduardo exhaled looking around.

"Are you okay?" Blas said.

"Yeah, how long does it take? Before you feel it?" Eduardo asked.

"Tranquílate, hermano." Blas stopped and placed his hand on Eduardo's shoulder. "It depends on the person. And it's subtle for everyone. The children have their own message for you. They will let you know. Just let them guide you. But, I would say about an hour."

One lap turned into another. And then another. And then another. Eduardo turned to Blas.

"Anything? I feel like it's been an hour."

"Just have patience," Blas said. "This one must be a longer journey. Are you doing okay?"

"Yeah, I'm fine. I guess I'm okay. I just feel, well, I feel like, I don't know." Eduardo turned to Blas. "I'm feeling a little down."

"That's okay. That's normal. No judgment of self. Los niños santos can show us many sides of ourselves. Sometimes we're not prepared to see those sides. These ones must be showing you—"

"No, I mean, I'm really feeling down, man. Like the blues. Like the depresh."

Blas faced Eduardo, took hold of his friend's shoulders, held him gently. "You're going to be fine. The first part is always the most challenging. You have to just surrender to it. You have to know that you're going to be fine."

Saying this, Blas knew something wasn't right. They should be feeling something—anything—by now. He searched for an answer. They'd been too active earlier. They ate the wrong food. They were metabolizing too slowly. Or, worse, the children had lost their potency. Or, the worst of all, the children were dead. He was certainly not feeling less a man and more a god. He was feeling just like a man. He thought of what don Luis would say. Don Luis would laugh. He would say they weren't ready. He would say los niños santos can do that to you. Don't take it personally. Take nothing personally.

Eduardo walked ahead. He picked up his step. Blas remembered this was another one of Eduardo's coping mechanisms. When he felt uncomfortable or didn't want to be somewhere, he picked up his pace. He turned tail and ran. He walked off stage. He cried when drunk.

"Eddie, look," Blas said, running up to him, "I think these might be duds. I hate to say it, but I think we might have the night off." Blas laughed uncomfortably.

"It's fine, it's fine," Eduardo said.

"Where are you going?"

"Back to the apartment. No, you know what, I'm going to call my—" Eduardo fished out his phone and checked the time. "Fuck, it's too late."

"What, what were you—"

"I was going to call my therapist. I just need to talk to someone."

"Eddie, don't do that, I'm right here. Let's just go back, you can take your meds, we'll just…watch a movie. Or let's go out. Puro party. Like the old days. I'll drink tonight."

Blas stopped, checked himself. *Were these things kicking in? No, no, they're not working. They're bunk. They're shit, oh shit, am I having a bad trip? Oh fuck. No, no, I'm not. These are shit.*

"Okay, okay," Blas shouted to Eduardo. "Just call me, let me know you made it. Please. I'm going to stay out here. I'm hoping these will start working."

"Bye, I gotta go. I feel like shit," Eduardo said, and then he was gone into the darkness. Blas had a feeling, a terrible one, that something bad was going to happen. That Eduardo would wander off into the dark and fall, or head for the river and try to jump in, or have a panic attack. Wait, that's what was happening. Eduardo was having a panic attack. He'd seen it once, a day or two before Eduardo's wedding. The night before the rehearsal dinner in Santa Fe. They were all out, all the families, the friends, the cousins. The band. Eduardo kept complaining about an upset stomach and was pacing at El Paseo, like he couldn't calm down. He kept complaining and in the bathroom he pulled Blas aside and said he didn't know if he could do it. That he'd be a terrible husband.

"You love each other," Blas had said. "You're exactly where you're supposed to be."

"She's never seen me like this. She doesn't know what she's in for. Oh my god, oh my god."

"Ed, she knows who you are. She loves you and she'll be there for you. Sickness and health."

Then his sister Ana just barged into the bathroom and grabbed him.

"Come on, Eddie" she said.

"What's going on?" I asked her.

Panic attack. She mouthed the words. They disappeared and everyone kept hanging out and partying, even the bride-to-be, Stella, like nothing happened. Two days later, they were married at Our Lady of Guadalupe Church, where Blas and Eduardo had made their First Communions in third grade.

Blas ran after him in the dark park, but stayed just far enough behind so Eduardo didn't hear him. Eduardo turned toward a small convenience store and it appeared he was going to go in, but he kept walking. Then he turned around and paced. Oh, shit, panic attack.

Eduardo sat down on the curb, a street lamp shining a cone of light over him. He began to cry. Blas couldn't watch this, he had to do something. He had to take him in, he had to go get his meds or something. He was about to dart toward Eduardo, but Eduardo stood up, and ran off, again into the darkness.

Blas tried Eduardo's phone. Straight to voicemail. He found his way back to Eduardo's apartment, only to find all the lights off, beds empty. No sigh of him. Blas left to search for Eduardo. The night dragged on, and Blas kept walking, checking his phone every so often. He even called Eduardo's name. So much for Hercules Martinez. He had no way of calling don Luis. No way of texting him a question about what to do. There was no Wi-Fi in San Jose del Pacifico. Don Luis checked email when he went into Puerto Escondido, which was once every few weeks.

About midnight, a text.

Eduardo: I'm back. Can you come?

Blas: Be right there

Eduardo was in bed. He was showered, calm. He was curled in the fetal position.

"Hey buddy, are you okay?" Blas knelt down to face his friend.

"Why did she leave me?" Eduardo said.

"Shhhh…" Blas said. "She's a puta, that's why."

"Fuck you, man," Eduardo said. "I loved her."

"Just trying to lighten the mood. I was worried. Where'd you go? Let me make some tea."

"Blas, just shut up for a little bit. Do you hear me? Just shut up."

Blas sat back on his ankles.

"I don't need you to do anything, okay?" Eduardo said. "I just need you to be my friend. Not my healer, not my shaman or whatever. Just be my friend."

It hit Blas all at once. It hit him like the time don Luis pulled him from the hot steamy temazcal, heaving for air, about to pass out, Luis dousing him with cold water from a hose. Or when he ate his first button of peyote and threw up so bad, don Luis had to slap him, then make him drink manzanilla tea to calm his stomach. Luis kept telling him he wasn't ready, that it would take years. Maybe Luis had sent him with dead children after all to teach him a lesson. Whatever the case, Blas knew he was doing this all wrong. What kind of healer was he? An amateur. A sorcerer's apprentice who had forgotten the true first rule: They call you. Not you call them.

Blas stood, took off his bandana and bracelets, untied the sash. He kicked his shoes off and pushed them all aside.

"You dressed under there?" he said.

"Yes, you dumbass. Boxer shorts," Eduardo said. "Get in here."

Blas complied, obeyed his friend's request. He nuzzled in behind Eduardo, his chin just barely touching his friend's shoulder. Eduardo took Blas's arm and draped it over his own body and exhaled as though it was his last breath. Blas did the same, and before long, they were both asleep.

CIRCLE OF DEATH

Dominic slowed his thrusting hips, shifted his weight onto his left elbow, and then whispered into Elisabeta's ear, "Get on top of me." She obliged, and as they switched positions, she now setting the pace of their passion, he sighed in relief as the horrendous pinch in his right shoulder eased, cuing his loins to fully relax.

"I'm coming," he said.

"Me, too." she whispered.

Elisabeta dug her fingernails into his pectorals, continuing to grind on top of him, until she gasped, Dominic arching his back about to moan. She placed her hand over his mouth.

"Shhh," she said, then fell on top of him, the moisture of their skin mixing into a potent fragrance.

She kissed him and lingered for a moment, her delicate round face illuminated by a faint red hue seeping in through the blinds of the dark trailer, its source the circles of the Target logo just across the lot.

"What is it?" Dominic asked. "Was it good?"

"I like it when you finish on top." She kissed him again, running her hand through his hair.

"I know." He smiled, patting her bottom. "I just needed…a rest tonight."

"You're tired. I know," she said.

"Well, my body's not cooperating."

"I think it's cooperating perfectly." Elisabeta ran her hand down his side body, making him shiver.

He laughed, but it was forced. He was in terrible pain.

"It's my shoulder," he said.

"Still?" she raised her head, concerned. "You need to see Sally."

"She just tells me to rest it, ice it."

"I think you should see a doctor," she said.

"When? How? Where are we now? San Bernardino?"

"Fontana, I think," she said.

"And then another city, and another city, and another," he said.

Elisabeta rolled off of him, curled into his big arms. She squeezed one, went *mmm*, running her hands over his chest and abdomen again. He was used to her requesting a second round, sometimes a third, and as much as he'd like to, he wasn't ready, his thoughts clouded by worry.

"You'll be fine," she said.

"Yeah."

But this time, he didn't know. His body was telling him something different. It wasn't healing like other injuries, the ones where he could indeed rest and ice, maybe take a day off. This was deep inside and it wasn't improving. He reached for his headphones. It was time for Bob, time to request a sleep time.

"Are you just going to sleep?" Elisabeta asked.

"If I can. I haven't been sleeping well these nights."

"You really are in pain," she said. She ran her hand over his nakedness, holding him in her hand. "I can help you fall asleep."

He sighed, smiled. "If you do all the work."

"Here." She took his headphones, placed them over his ears, then handed him his phone. He unlocked it, tapped his music, pulling up "Three Little Birds," by Bob Marley and The Wailers. He opened the Slumbr app and requested Stage 1 NREM in twenty minutes. The app offered back twenty-five minutes, thirty minutes, or he could pay extra for a fifteen-minute start time.

"Too many people on," he said, and hit play before tossing the phone aside.

"Don't worry," she said, straddling him, "you don't need that anyway. It's addictive. I'll get you to sleep."

Before anything happened, a bang on the trailer door interrupted them. Elisbeta jumped off Dominic, reaching for covers and her clothes.

"My father," she whispered.

"Open up in there," the voice said.

Dominic slid his right earmuff back. "It's Milos," he assured Elisabeta. "Come in. Wait, hold on."

He sat up helping Elisabeta find her clothes, while he put on shorts.

"Okay, now," he said.

The door opened. It was Milos. Strong Man number two. Dominic's partner in the Circle of Death, the second runner up of Cedros Circus most fit men.

"Don't do that!" Elisabeta said.

"You're fine. Your parents' trailer is dark. Everyone's asleep. Except you two. Is he being nice to you?" Milos leaned in to kiss Elisabeta on the cheek.

"He's hurt," she said.

"What did you do to him?" Milos said.

"His shoulder," she said.

"Oh, yeah. That," Milos said.

"You know?" she said.

"We're roommates. I know everything about this guy."

"Tell him he needs to go to the doctor." Elisabeta stood in front of a small mirror above their sink, fixing her hair.

"Dominic, go to the doctor."

"You asshole," she said.

"D, I need to go to bed," Milos said. "You two…done?"

Dominic laid back down, put his headphones on. "Yeah."

"You two need to clean this place up," she said, leaning down to kiss Dominic.

He woke his phone again. "Yes!" he said. "There's one in ten minutes."

"Hey, before you drift off there, lover boy," Milos said, "Gus needs us up early tomorrow. He's sending us to Home Depot for sawdust."

"Fuck," Dominic sat up, wincing. "More rain tomorrow?"

"Yeah," Milos said. "We have to prepare the arena."

"Goodnight, boys," Elisabeta said.

"See you tomorrow." Dominic blew her a kiss. Milos blew her a kiss, too.

Dominic pressed play again. The badda-bop-bop of the snare, followed by the electric organ, kicked off his Marley song for the millionth time. His Slumbr would be there soon.

Rise up this morning,
Smile at the rising sun,
Three little birds,
Each by my doorstep…

Dominic awoke with a gasp. Bob Marley still playing in his headset. This had happened before, as though he just stopped breathing, but those other times it was in the middle of the night, without the use of the app, when he used to fall asleep on his own. Now, the sky was still dark, the overcast thicker with the heavy clouds above threatening rain. Their trailer door opened quietly, the blinds hitting the small window as Silvia slipped in. She was a leg artist from Valencia, Spain, who twirled towels on her toes. She was ten years his senior, and in love with Dominic, one, because he spoke Spanish to her.

Theirs, however, was transactional. A mutual bodily agreement; some sort of care treaty. She was the taker, he was the giver. This morning, as she crawled over him, trying not to wake Milos, peeling covers and underwear off Dominic, he said to her, "Rápido, por favor."

She tried to kiss his belly moving further down toward his waking member, but he shook his head and took her hand, placing it around him, guiding her to work him this way.

"Qué lindo," she said. "Está bien." She settled in next to him, at first in the hook of his right arm, but he moved her to the left side of his body.

"Mi hombro," he said, but she was busy now, and Milos, on the other bed, was waking up. He popped his head up for a moment, rolled his eyes, then turned the other direction. After Dominic's climax, Silvia came in for a kiss, which Dominic returned, then when she put her breasts in his face, he did what she loved: kissing them, rubbing his stubble on her soft skin and nipples, sucking. She attempted to take the rest of her clothes off, but he pointed at Milos.

"Entonces, ya me voy," she said, gathering herself.

"Sí, temenos que trabajar."

"Más tarde?" She shrugged, tied her coat closed.

"Si tú quieres."

"Si, te queiro." Silvia slipped out.

Milos turned over.

"Bro, you have a rough life," he said, rubbing his eyes.

Dominic stood up, cleaned himself, pulled his shorts up.

"Looks that way," Dominic said. "But is this it?"

"What do you mean?"

A banging at their door interrupted their conversation.

"You girls decent? You two better not be making out in there?" Gus, the superintendent, was inappropriate with everyone, but then again, who wasn't at Cedros Circus? There were no such things as sexual harassment trainings or codes of team sensitivity.

"Gus," Milos said.

Gus pushed his way inside their trailer. Himself a retired strong man, he began barking orders.

"I went this morning and bought the sawdust already. It's in the truck. You're welcome. After that, go help Lety at the ticket booth. She wants to move a filing cabinet or some shit. Just go over there."

Gus pointed at them, the only way he communicated, with a finger out and waving followed by commands. "And what's with you this morning?" Gus cocked his chin at Dominic. "You're always wearing those headphones. You avoiding something?"

"Tired," Dominic said. "And my shoulder."

"Go see Sally." Gus snapped his fingers. "We've got a big crowd today. It's already raining."

Tossing sawdust solidified what kind of act they were. They were plastic bucket seats and wooden gangways, that, when it rained, needed sawdust to absorb the moisture so the audience wouldn't slip on the way to their seats.

Pausing to look back at their work in the arena, Dominic exhaled with effort.

"We're slaves here. We're like pieces of meat. People just come to take a slice of us."

"That's what the circus is," Milos said. "We're performers."

"But what about Las Vegas? Think about it. O. Zumanity. The audience comes in dressed up, sits on velvet seats. They order a cocktail. Not hot dogs and popcorn that we have to sell them during intermission. Their feet aren't covered in sawdust."

"Well, go try out for them. What's stopping you?" Milos said.

Dominic fell silent. He turned to his friend, and decided then and there to say it.

"I think I'm done."

"With performing?"

"Yes, with everything. I can't go on. My shoulder. I think it's ruined."

"Don't go on today. Rest," Milos said. "Pavel can do Circle of Death with me."

"I think I can still do Circle of Death," Dominic said.

Milos held his arms up over his head.

"Grab my forearms and push as hard as you can," he said.

Dominic followed his friend's command, but the mere act of lifting his right arm made him wince, and then pushing against Milos' frame hurt him even more.

"You can't," Milos said. "You'll fall off."

"I'm going to try."

Milos shook his head.

After costumes and make up, fifteen minutes before curtain, Dominic and Milos stood at the Selfie Station to pose with a line of guests, most of them teenage girls with their phones. They snapped pictures of the men, then moved in next to them, some giggling, others shy. One girl asked to squeeze Dominic's bicep. He flexed for her as she held the phone out in front of them.

In between pictures, Milos whispered, "Did you talk to Pavel?"

"No. I will be fine," Dominic said.

"Gus doesn't like surprises," Milos said.

He couldn't ask Pavel. Dominic suspected Pavel was on to him about sleeping with his daughter, Elisabeta, and Pavel could squash him barehanded. Even at fifty-five-years-old, Pavel was still the strongest of them all; he'd been hoisting up his family of four while mounted on a unicycle most of his adult life.

Backstage, the call bell rang. Two minutes to showtime. Everyone circled up, began hugging and cheek kissing, giving high fives and butt slaps, making signs of the cross, holding hands in prayer, jumping and prancing and flourishing in place. The players encircled the clowns, who would run and skip and unicycle out into the arena the instant the music started. After that, the Pageant of Flags. Elisabeta would hold Romania's, Milos Ukraine's, Silvia Spain's and Dominic, USA's. At the flag bucket, choosing their colors, Dominic and Elisabeta's eyes met. She smiled.

"I need talk to your father," Dominic said.

Her mild coquette turned to concern. "Why?"

"Where is he?" Dominic said, thinking about how much he needed to rest. He loved how the Slumbr app just pulled away all that anxiety and worry as you drifted off to sleep, so peaceful and easy. If he could just…

"I need to ask him—" Dominic's eyes darted around the melee. The bass drum and high hat cymbals, followed by the brass and organ, erupted in an ecstatic fury piped in from an audio track—Cedros Circus had let go of their orchestra years ago. Gus drew an imaginary circle in the air with his thick forefinger. The clowns, never truly out of character, whooped and yipped and burst through the curtain. It was a full house despite the rain. They could still sell out a matinee.

Out on pageant, flags held high, the smell of wet sawdust bothered Dominic's nose. He held his flag lower than usual, even the fiberglass flagstaff irritated his shoulder. The music had morphed into a march of sorts, a vague but majestic mash up of national anthems. They all took their positions in the ring as the music crescendo-ed. Master Jack De Carlo took the floor, hopping onto the round platform in the middle.

"Ladies and gentlemen, boys and girls…," he said.

Backstage, the players scattered to their corners and seats. Silvia and black-clad stagehands turned back toward the curtain. Dominic caught her gazing eyes as he continued to look for Pavel. She winked at him, and in his distraction, he returned a half-hearted wave. She stuck her nose up at him, then strutted out to perform the opening act.

The Amazing Georgescu's—sisters Roxana, Stefania, and their mother Maria practiced throwing rings. Missing from this party was Elisabeta and Pavel. Dominic approached the family, and before he could inquire where Pavel might be, their father himself marched straight toward them, Elisabeta at his side, timid against her tank of a father. His usual jolly strength carried a cloud over it.

"You," he said, approaching Dominic.

"Pavel, I need to ask you something. I need your—"

"My what? My blessing? Elisabeta told me."

"Told you what?"

"That you two...are together."

Elisabeta stood behind her father.

"No, that's not what I—look, I can't go on today. I'm injured. Can you do Circle of Death?"

"I see you around here," Pavel leaned in over Dominic. "The pretty boy flexing for everyone. I see how these women throw themselves at you."

Dominic backed away. Pavel grabbed him by the shoulders.

"If you touch her again—"

Dominic grimaced, trying not to scream, his knees buckling.

"Stop, please." Dominic cried out, attempting to wiggle out of Pavel's grip. Milos had come to the commotion, tried to help Dominic, but backed off as Pavel shot him a glare.

"Please," Dominic said. "I can't go on."

"Tata, please, stop." Elisabeta stepped out from beside her father.

Gus approached them, pulled his headset off his ear.

"What the fuck is going on here?"

"Dominic is hurt," Elisabeta said.

"I came to ask Pavel to do Circle of Death," Dominic said, now free from Pavel's hands.

"He's hurt, Gus. He can't perform," Milos said.

"You can't make changes like this, buddy." Gus threw his hands up, then pointed at Dominic. "You know what, get the hell out of here. Go see Sally."

Dominic rubbed his shoulder backing away from the scene. Out in the arena, the crowd clapped and cheered, the music intensifying by the second. Dominic looked back, met Elisabeta's eyes. She shrugged, shook her head. Milos patted Dominic's back.

"You'll be fine," Milos said.

But Dominic wouldn't. He'd never be again. He trudged from the inner workings under the tent, down another soggy sawdust gangway to the cast exit, out to the trailers. Sad Sack stood there just at the exit, halfway in, halfway out, avoiding a complete drenching as the rain hadn't let up. He'd stopped wearing full make up years ago, and now opted for spiky bleached hair and baggy surfer wear, his ample gut holding it all up. He still painted on his signature frown, a kind of downtrodden Guy Fieri trapped at the circus. Dominic walked into one of Sad Sack's cigarette exhales.

"Hey Sam." Dominic coughed. "I mean, Sad Sack."

Sad Sack shrugged. "Can't be in character all the time, you know what I mean?"

The clown exhaled.

"What's with you?" he said.

"My shoulder—it's—" Dominic's chin quivered.

"It's okay, kid. You're young," Sad Sack said. "Smoke?"

Dominic waved it off and moved along, wiping rain off his brow, his perfect hair now flat.

Sally's trailer was half athletic trainer's lab, half circus museum, all hoarder. She was great for taping and stretching and icing, but a doctor she was not. At least not the medical kind. Performers were known to spend a few minutes in her trailer, or a few hours. Her brusque demeanor and sturdy build belied a sweet side, a tenderness that was there but rarely seen.

"Let's see," she said, waving Dominic inside. "And shut that door. It's cold."

No need to take off his leather vest. He simply pointed.

"I was wondering when you were going to come in," she said, pressing about his shoulder with gingerly finesse. "Does it hurt when I do this?"

She lifted his arm, light as air, and gently twisted it so his thumb turned inward and down. Dominic screamed.

"You waited too long to see me, sweetie." She tutted. "It's your rotator. I can't do anything for it. We have to get you to orthopedics."

His eyes warmed and tears gathered, pooling at his lower eyelids. He started to shudder and rubbed at his eyes. Sally turned away to the kitchen space, opened her refrigerator, and gathered supplies. She swung back to him, gave him a tissue.

"Your eyeliner's smearing," she said, then went to affixing bags of ice to his shoulder, wrapping them to his bare skin.

"This is—this is…" Dominic was sobbing now.

"The worse thing that's ever happened to you?" She finished wrapping him, then gave him two white tablets and a cup of water.

"Yes, yes it is," he said. "Are these for sleep?"

"No, for pain. But I hear a lot of you kids use that sleep app. Thing will destroy you if you're not careful. Take them now, then go to sleep. On your own. Not that stupid app. Kids calling for a sleep time like it's goddamn car ride."

"But the show."

"Oh, you're not doing the show, honey. Not today, not for a while. You're going to need surgery. Months of rehab."

"This is my life," he said.

"I know. And life is now telling you to do something different." Sally leaned against the sink, crossed her arms, her tattoo sleeves on full display. "I know what you're going through. I was an acrobat. Trapeze artist. I was good, then I took a fall, fucked up my hip, never got up there again."

She caressed her forearm ink.

"Then I started getting these beauties. I used to run with a circus where they had a side show. I became the Tattooed Lady. *Lydia, oh, Lydia, oh have you met Lydia, Lydia the tattooed lady.* You know that song? *When her robe's unfurled, she'll show you the world...* No? Anyway, in my tent, I'd stand around in a bikini and flex. In another corner was a pit of snakes, and in another corner was this poor little girl who had no arms, cute little thing. What was her name? Amy? Amanda? Anyway, she could feed herself a banana with her feet. I had a rocking body back then. I was built like a shit brick house.

"Thing was I couldn't quit the circus. It was just in me, but I couldn't pay the bills getting tatted up and posing all day, and besides, everyone started getting tattoos so it wasn't so exotic. So, I became an athletic trainer to take care of you kids. What I'm saying, handsome, is you have to change. Reinvent. It'll make you stronger."

"What am I going to do? This is all I know," Dominic said.

"Quit being so melodramatic," she said. "Stand around and look pretty. Become an underwear model for all I care. Either way, you're going to have to do something different. At least for a while. Or get that wing back to work and get up there and fly again. Go get some rest. Then come back and we'll put some heat on it."

Dominic left her trailer, paused and looked up at the sky. He had heard somewhere that you could set the Slumbr app to put you into a permanent sleep. A suspended animation. Not quite death, but not *not* death. That sounded good right now. A long, forever rest. The rain had slowed but he was still shuddering. Right now, there was no one to show off for, to flex for, or to demonstrate his might. The act was over.

He was going to head back to his trailer when Elisabeta turned up walking toward him, sparkling in her sequins, shielded by a dainty umbrella. A spark of hope hit his stomach. She approached him with caution.

"Are you okay?" she said.

"It's my rotator cuff. I'm ruined."

"I'm sorry about my father," she said. "I didn't mean for that to happen. I thought you were going to tell him about you and me, so I told him. I wanted him to hear it from me."

"That's fine. It doesn't matter."

"You're crying." She reached for him, laid a hand on his cheekbone.

"Don't you have to get in there?" he said, wiping his face.

"In a few minutes," she said. "I just wanted to check on you."

He reached for her hand.

"So, now that your dad knows, how about we spend more time working on you and me," he said.

Elisabeta drew her hand in.

"What do you mean, you and me?" she said.

"I thought—we—well, that we have something. You come visit me almost every day." He smiled.

"There is no you and me," she said. "And others visit you, too. It's no secret." She looked away.

"Oh, I just thought we—"

"No," she said, "and I'm leaving the circus."

In place of the hope he had felt moments before, a punch of dread hit him in the abdomen.

"What will you do?" he asked.

"I want to go to university."

"University? Like college?"

"The circus isn't for me anymore," she said.

"But what about your family. It's your act."

"It's theirs. Not mine," she said.

"Where are you going to college?" he said.

"I want to go back to Romania. I want to study to be a doctor there."

His stomach sunk again. A shockwave of pain took over him, as though his shoulder had spread its ache to all the neurons in his body. He felt paralyzed. Off to their left, a banner advertising Cedros Circus affixed to a utility trailer showed the silhouette of the strong man, one arm up holding a barbell, the other arm akimbo. Sally was right, this was the worst thing that had ever happened to him.

"I have to go," Elisabeta said.

"Break a leg," he said.

"You Americans and your superstitions," she said.

"Good luck," she said to him, waving, then ducking into the tent.

Good luck, he whispered back.

In his trailer, Dominic almost tapped the Slumbr icon, but instead opened a chat and asked the bot to provide a list of the dangers of the Slumbr app. Among other things, prolonged usage could cause muscle atrophy, skeletal damage, inflammation, neurological damage. The bot asked if there was anything else it could help with. He bit his lip. Fuck. He hovered his finger over his music, then stopped. He then asked it for a list of orthopedic surgeons in his hometown of Salinas. Then, he opened another window and typed Cirque de Soleil. Tapped on Careers.

"CHAERONEA EVE"

Akakios stepped into the candle-lit bed chamber, covered only by his tunic, which fell to the middle of his muscular thighs. The white cotton crepe hugged his chest and was cinched at his waist by a single gold braid, tied at his belly button. On the bed, covered by a sheet up to his waist lie Damon, the thick dark curls on his head starting to show the first grays, his ample chest already covered thick by even numbers of white and black hair.

"Come." Damon motioned to Akakios, holding his hand out, waiting for his *erômenos* to take it.

"Shall we bathe?" Akakios said, taking Damon's hand.

"Yes, beloved. Lead me."

The boy servants had poured the last of the pitchers of hot water into the bath and took their leave, letting the warriors alone. At the tiled ledge of the bath, they faced each other, Damon, just a brow taller than Akakios, held his sheet at his waist and stared into the young man's eyes. Damon let his sheet drop, revealing the rest of his thick muscled frame, dusted with hair. With his eyes still fixed on Akakios' blue irises, Damon untied the cord around Akakios' waist, letting it fall to the tiles. Then, he took the bottom of Akakios' tunic and lifted it up *daktylos* by *daktylos*. Once the white fabric was over Akakios' head, Damon dropped the tunic to the floor and admired his beloved's body.

"You have gained much muscle in these last few weeks," Damon said.

"We have to be prepared," Akakios said. "Alexander and the Macedon army are fierce. He will stop at nothing."

"Shhh…" Damon reached down between Akakios' thighs. He took hold and began to caress the young man. Akakios gasped, restraining himself from touching Damon. With his other hand, Damon fondled Akakios' chin, fingering the sparse beard of his young lover. Damon increased his intensity and grip on Akakios' phallus until he felt moisture. Akakios threw his head back, but then corrected, returning his gaze back to Damon's.

Damon stopped his work, then gathered his sheet at his knees on which he knelt, his nose nearly touching the *posthe* of Akakios' rigidness.

"But my love, we're not to—" Akakios whispered.

"We shall not, but you look so delicious now, I must have a taste of your sweet skin."

Damon leaned forward, breaking most of the covenants, and opened his mouth, enveloping Akakios, while grabbing the young man's backside to pull him deeper inside. Damon buried his lips and nose in the musk of Akakios' smallest curls, his dried sweat still salty and pleasingly acrid from their last practice battle that afternoon. Akakios moaned. Damon released his hands from Akakios' buttocks and took Akakios' hands dangling at this side, then set them on Damon's own head, lacing his lover's fingers into his head curls, commanding in silence for his erômenos to take over. Akakios understood what to do, and so he pulled Damon's face and mouth back and forth on his phallus until he was on the verge of release.

"But lover, um, we're not to—" Akakios said, trying to lift Damon up.

Damon released his lips and breathed then stood, meeting Akakios' eyes once more. Damon squeezed Akakios down there to make sure he had not lost his sacredness, that Akakios had controlled himself as he was supposed to, saving the warm sweetness for the following night whence they would return to this same chamber to seal their lust in earnest following a defeated Macedon army.

In the bath, they faced each other, soaped one another, then shaved. Akakios shaving Damon first: cheeks, mustache, preserving his beard, then onto Damon's chest and legs. Damon returned the favor taking his time grooming Akakios. After, they dried each other off, then applied olive oil onto each other's bodies.

"I cannot wait to have you again," Akakios said. "The way you took me in your mouth."

"I want you again," Damon said. "Now."

"May I?" Akakios looked down below Damon's waist.

"You must," Damon said.

Akakios returned the ritual for his *erastês*, reaching for Damon's oiled phallus, tugging it forward and back with one hand, while his other hand caressed Damon's jawline. Damon, unable to control himself, stepped forward, grabbing Akakios' hips, pulling his beloved to him so their thighs touched.

"Let us prepare our dress for tomorrow," Akakios said, pulling away, taking Damon's hand, leading him to their dressing table. Before them lay their tunics, and breastplates, their shin greaves and helmet. Damon grunted, shook his head no, but Akakios turned his attention to their armor.

"I shall wake first, then wake you. I will drape this over you." Akakios took Damon's tunic from the table and pulled it over

Damon's shoulders and down his body. Damon allowed it wiggling back into the tunic with impatience.

"I'm not sure that I can wait," Damon said.

"Let us dress from head to toe, then undress one another, and then you can have me. You can have all of me," Akakios turned to his hoplite laid out with precision by the servant boys, and then began to dress, tunic over himself, shin greaves and helmet. "Let's dress now."

"No, I'm serious. I—I can't wait. Adam, I'm going to come," Dave said, now out of his Damon character.

"Right now?" Adam said. Akakios gone from scene.

"I just—oh God, hold on." Damon fell back onto the bed, climaxing. The tunic caught the ejaculate. "Fuck. Now we have to wash these. We can't return these with cum stains."

Adam, helmeted, and half-dressed tried to help Dave out of the tunic.

"No, I got, I got it." Dave said. He pulled the tunic off, tossed it in his dirty clothes pile. Will you start these? I'm going to take a shower."

"A shower?" Adam said. "Now? We just took a bath."

"Yeah. I need to wash this off."

"Just wipe it off." Adam said. "And hey, I was just getting going. I need to shoot one, too."

"Well, then do it. I mean, I blew you already," Dave said.

"Yeah, but you didn't let me come."

"That's because we were in fucking character." Dave threw his hands up and stormed back into to the bathroom

"Fuck," he said. The tub is full. And all of our hair is floating in it. Damn it."

Adam met him in the bathroom.

"I mean, how long do we have to keep…never mind…" Dave leaned over to drain the tub.

"Look, I just. I can't do the role play," Dave said. My ex-wife was into that and I wasn't and—it's probably what drove us apart…"

"Are you embarrassed about the…" Adam took the helmet off.

"About the what?" Dave said.

"The premature…" Adam trailed off.

"No." Dave watched the water swirl down the drain. He turned on the shower. "Well, that's part of it. It's just—"

"I can't hear you," Adam said. "Turn off the water. Please."

"I don't—I don't want to do role play or dress up. I mean these scripts you wrote up? We had to rehearse this shit? I just want to fuck, okay? I'm too old for this. I'm too old as it is. I just want to get my rocks off and just get on with it."

"Your rocks?" Adam laughed a bit.

"Or whatever you guys call it. Whatever slang you use. I shouldn't even be seeing you."

"Because I'm young?" Adam said.

"Yes. I'm old. I should be…"

"With another old dude?" Adam said. "Look, I like you. I like older men. You turn me on. You're my fantasy, and I thought you might like this. Just something different. Because—I don't know—every time we've been together, I just feel kinda…used."

Dave, in his nakedness, suddenly felt exposed. He grabbed a towel and wrapped himself.

"I don't know if I'm going to stay here tonight," Adam said.

"No, just stop," Dave said. "I'm sorry if I—make you feel that way. This is still all very new for me. I don't even know what I'm doing. Or if what I'm doing is right."

"Oh no, you are," Adam said. "All right, look. Have a good night. Just call me. And I'll take care of the costumes, okay? Take your shower."

Adam left the bathroom. Dave followed him.

"Wait." Dave turned to the dresser where they had laid out the costumes. He shuffled through the scripts Adam had wrote. He found his line.

"Akakios," he continued. "Please dress your *erastês*."

"Come on, dude, mood has passed," Adam said, getting his regular clothes on, shoes already on feet.

Dave, now Damon, dropped his towel and ran his fingers delicately over the plumes of his helmet. "We must practice tonight once more. I had a vision that tomorrow we will all die. That we and all the Sacred Band will succumb to Alexander."

"Is that so?" Adam laughed a bit.

Dave glanced at the papers once more, but then marched past them.

"What you are you doing here, young man?" Dave said. "Are you a traveler from the future? You look lost. And what is this modern attire? I wish to see what is under it. May I?"

ANIMAL HUSBANDRY

The thing was, was that they kept different hours. But this was nothing new. Rose was a confirmed night owl and Mario was an early bird, or, as he called himself, an anytime bird. He claimed he was alert any time of day, but he was always inclined to go to bed early, and now in midlife, there was rarely a night when he wasn't "lights out" by 10 p.m.

"Over time you learn that people are the way they are and they're not apt to change," was what Antoinette Felix had said to him on a Zoom call when she was letting him know the bad news. Mario couldn't remember the context of her comment, but when she said it, he was thinking of his wife, Rose, and that she would probably be a late-nighter for life. Antoinette Felix, Mario's regional VP, talked in those pithy one-liners that revealed both universal truths and her own problems at home at the same time.

The bad news: Mario's position, along with twenty-seven others like him across the country, was eliminated. Gone, in what felt like a snap, yet it wasn't that much of a surprise. Mario's insider friend from another division, Gary Aronson, said to be prepared. Gary knew everything and everybody and so when, two weeks before Antoinette's call, Gary's position was eliminated too, Gary's last words to Mario were, "I told you so." Followed by, "We just can't compete."

With the machines, is what Gary meant. The bots had at last come for sales. Who knew that this would ever happen? People would always feel more comfortable interacting with humans. Always. But first it was the prospect emails, then the follow up emails, then the creation of sales plans and strategic monthly reports that came easier for the bots. They learned it all and rendered people like Mario and Gary and all the others whose livelihood was built on relationships with humans, obsolete. He had sensed something was on the horizon; he just didn't know that he was going to lose everything to a chat feature with the verbal aptitude of a high school junior.

"It's not so bad," Rose said over dinner that night. "At least they gave you a package."

"But that's just for a few months. We'll make it to September at best." Mario began clearing the table, rinsing plates, and putting them in the dishwasher. Their tween daughters, Becca and Bella had retreated to their tablets, a place where they zoned out. It was a refuge for ignoring their parents when the bickering started. It was never long before that happened. Tonight, it was more Cold War-style. Few words, lots of tension. Passive aggression on point. Mario was an expert at this, but Rose was the Supreme Master of Icy Relations.

"I'll do those," she said.

"I got it," he said, his sink work quicker, water splashing as he moved dishes from sink to rack. He was thinking of what to say, how to say that they would need to figure something out soon. How the severance wasn't going to last, how her work as a party planner was probably doomed too with the rise of the ... Intelligencia, he sometimes called it. And he also wanted to have a philosophical talk with her, just some time to speculate and ponder, however that was never on the table. She was known for shutting down conversations that flirted with the idea that there was life beyond the Solar System.

"How would we ever know?" she had said in their early courtship in response to Mario's, "The universe is much too big for us to be the only intelligent form of life in it." That was that. She had changed the subject to talk about cruises. She was crazy about cruises. He was not. They had met on a cruise years before, when travel was normal. Before the outbreaks and masks and political violence.

Tonight's silent battle wasn't based on anything in particular. It was a typical Tuesday. She'd just come from her telepathy classes, of which Mario thought they were getting longer each time. Their family calendar was populated with at least three a week. She had just switched teachers; evidently Google tapped the previous one to work on a new e-telepathy training program.

Telepathy being one of the few things the bots couldn't actually do. Telepathy, it was predicted, would be one of the most coveted job skills in the new economy. Mind reading was going to be the next indoor plumbing. Mario thought differently. You would know if you were a mind reader, wouldn't you? It's not something you could teach or learn. It was like his profession as a salesman—you either had it or you didn't. Plus, she was spending so much money on those classes.

That's what was bothering him, that and the fact that they hadn't had sex in—what was it, three, almost four months. This was typical. They'd go through long dry spells, then get back on and things would be fine, then more dry spells and so on. It wasn't good or bad. It was just—marriage. With kids. That, and they were busy people. Now that the Plague had passed, they were getting back into activities outside of the home that they had paused for a few years. He'd returned to the gym and was feeling more confident about his 45-year-old body. He was chipping away at the dad bod, at least one line of abs was starting to peek out again.

On those nights that they went to bed at different times, which was every night, Mario found himself spooning his Just-Like-Me body pillow. That was the other craze: these body pillows that were in your likeness. You could send in a picture of yourself and Just-Like-Me would mold and print a custom body pillow about a third of your size for you to cuddle. This came out of the Post-Plague mental and spiritual health surge in which everyone was devoted to self-care and rescuing their inner children. Rose had one made too, and they worked for a while, but then they became these strange doll-like creatures that hung around. Even Becca and Bella lost interest playing with their parents' mini-doppelgängers.

Mario knew it was a problem when he began having sex with Rose's pillow. He did it once as a little joke, something to make himself laugh, but there in the dark, it helped fill a void, and acheive the post-coital relief, the one that helped him nod off to sleep after a stressful day. It was also something different, something to break up the monotony. Something to ease the loneliness even though Rose was in the next room up pecking away on the computer, working on whatever it was she worked on so late into the night.

But then one night, he didn't know he was fucking his own pillow by accident, and it both grossed him out and made him think for a minute what it might be like to have sex with…himself. He pushed the pillows out of the bed and the next morning they were gone. Rose had bagged them and put them in the garage next to a pile of old pool noodles. When things disappeared in their home, they were usually in the garage.

"I'm going up to the hot tub," he said, after he finished washing the dishes. His shirt was soaked and so was the floor at his feet.

"Okay." Rose was in of those patterns where she neither agreed and nor disagreed. Her response was more of an agreement tinged with a question. *Okay?* Mario had learned to let those ones slide. She glanced at his shirt and the floor, her eyes communicating he needed to clean up the mess.

"Oh, can you change the cat litter?" Mario said before he went upstairs.

"Okay," she said, retreating to the couch with her phone. With the three of them on their devices like this, the house fell into an eerie calm, which often signaled to Mario that he could and should slip away. *They'll never know I'm gone.* He'd done it one time—just decided to take a walk on a Sunday afternoon when they were all deep into their screens—but when one of them, maybe Rose, maybe one of the girls sensed his absence, his phone lit up with a somewhat panicked tone. "Where are you? You can't just leave like that without telling us where you went."

And it's not like you don't spend hours—HOURS—outside of the home, and with your location finder off. And do I say a word? Do I ask?

Ten bucks says she doesn't change the litter, he thought walking up the stairs. He'd bet himself like that all the time about those stupid little domestic chores, and in doing so, his resentment account was overflowing.

Back downstairs, now in his swim trunks and draped in his fading blue terry cloth robe, Becca, the youngest, popped up from her tablet screen.

"I wanna come!"

"Oh no, honey, it's late. You have to get ready for bed."

Rose shot him a look. Yes, it was her night to put them to bed, but could he take them to the hot tub, too? Was that what the look meant? Was she using some of her new telepathy skills on him? She hadn't really told him anything about what she was learning in those classes.

"No, honey," Rose said to Becca. "It's bedtime soon."

"Okay, I'll be back," Mario said.

"Okay." This time was less inquiry, more feigned agreement dashed with offense. He couldn't read minds, but he certainly felt words. He locked on her nose, not her eyes, and not the space just between them as a potential protection from her third eye gazing into him. He almost laughed to himself: *can she actually read minds?*

The Ariana Community Clubhouse hot tub was hit or miss. Hit if you could get it alone, which was what Mario hoped for, and miss if there were people overstaying the recommended 30-minutes per group, plus, drinking, which was not allowed, but everyone did it. Not to mention, the tub only held a max of eight people. More than that and it became a disgusting bath with strangers, the water quickly turning a mucky green from all the people dipping without showering first.

Mario detested this more than anything. A former pool boy, he knew the fastest way to destroy a pool was to get in without rinsing off, the sweat and oils and laundry detergents that people carried into the water destroyed the chemical integrity, and thus created a breeding ground for bacteria. He was convinced it was how he caught molluscum contagiosum back in his single years, when he frequented his ex-girlfriend's upscale apartment jacuzzi, which was a festering hub for singles. Temptation Apartments, they used to call it.

At the Ariana Clubhouse, Mario went straight for the showers, and after he was doused in the cold water en route to the hot tub, he noticed activity—bodies moving against the high lights of the two pillar beacons on either side of the tub and the low lights of the bulbs inside the water, casting a warm glow upward into the cloudy dark blue sky. He considered turning away. He wanted only to relax, to think, to consider the future, the future him. He couldn't do that with people. He'd have to make small talk. The way these bodies were moving, the laughs he heard as he approached meant they were there for fun. And, once he was within fifteen feet, he realized it was *them*.

They were the neighbors from a few buildings down from his home. They were a couple. Or a throuple, a word he had learned in recent months. Or maybe they were a quadruple. At the very least, there was the man and the woman who were always hanging on each other. They were a young professional looking type but could also still be in college. Either way, they were young enough that their bodies were…perfect. With them was another young man, perhaps their roommate, and he usually had another girl with him—never the same one—or sometimes another friend, and those friends brought their friends.

Those friends were difficult to describe. One was most certainly male from the top up, but from the waist below, Mario didn't know. Once, on another pool visit, when Mario had brought his daughters, some of the Quadruple's friends were there doing yoga on the deck, while the others were laughing and splashing and hanging on each other. Mario found himself stealing glances at the ones whom he couldn't tell exactly what they were, wondering if their downward dogs would reveal what was actually between their legs. He'd snap away from his errant glances when one of his daughters called him, bringing him back to the reality that he was now that total pool perv, the type he used to silently chide when he worked at the YMCA eons ago.

But what was between people's legs didn't matter nowadays. It didn't matter who you were below your belt and who you were inside your head. He knew this from all the diversity training at work and the questions his daughters brought up about non-binary and what not. He wasn't exactly prepared to talk about these things with his young girls, but he wasn't exactly not prepared either. He simply hadn't formed a perspective yet, and he was a little unsure whether he should at all.

He kept walking toward the hot tub. It appeared to be only the main couple, the man and woman, plus their roommate, and what appeared to be another woman, though the roommate and the other woman were not too close to each other, not like the Core Couple, Mario had suddenly dubbed them in his mind as he was kicking off his Birkenstocks. He nodded toward all of them, signaling he was about to enter this adult soup.

The other person stealing glances was the roommate. Mario had sensed this young man's eyes once before on their street, either when one was driving into the circle or the other was walking or checking the mailbox. They seemed to be those innocuous neighborly glances when you look up and acknowledge the other person's existence and you either nod or smile or some other combination. But Mario had noticed a pattern with the young man where he seemed to be outside whenever Mario was outside. Once, the young man was walking to his car for work in the morning, and he looked up at Mario as though trying to get his attention. Mario disregarded those glances, thought they were nothing more than two neighbors who kept similar schedules.

Here, now at the hot tub, Mario saw those same inquisitive eyes from the young man, and he also felt them from the woman nearest to him. At first glance, Mario recognized her as another neighbor, but here in the dim lights her face blurred into the foamy surface, her focused eyes on him were the only visible feature.

"Hello." Mario gave a small wave as he eased into the hot water.

"Hi."

"What's up?"

The Core Couple tilted their chins at him. They were laughing about something mischievous it seemed.

"What do you think?" the girl said to the other two. "What do you think love is?"

The unrecognizable woman leaned forward, lighting up with a smile. Now Mario recognized her. She was the older woman on the far opposite end of his street who walked her dog in a stroller. He always scoffed to himself at this. *Why on earth would someone walk their dog in a stroller?*

"It's the one you want to share something with first," she said.

The young girl laughed. "What?"

"What I mean is, when you see or experience something new or exciting, who's the first person you want to share it with? That person, that's the person you love. That first person you think of. That's what love is."

They all laughed. "What do you think?"

Mario didn't realize they were asking him until the male roommate turned to Mario.

"Hey," the roommate said, "They're asking what you think love is."

"Oh, me?" Mario heard it all, but was pretending not to be seen. And come to think of it, he didn't have a first person whom he thought of when he experienced something cool. Rose didn't come to mind because these days when he shared anything with her, she was aloof at best. Maybe he shared things with Gail first. She was his direct teammate and together they were a pair of gossips. Gail was also let go. She and Mario were texting all that morning, commiserating the company's ridiculous decision.

"Yeah," the girl in the Core Couple asked, "What do you think love is?"

Mario smiled at them looking for a witty response.

"I think…love is…a figment of our imaginations."

"Whoa!" the Core Couple man said. "Deep!"

The bathers laughed and Mario joined them, but he wasn't trying to be funny. He really meant it. Everything those days was made up. It was all imagined. The difficulty was, he didn't know whose imagination it was coming from. Humans or the machines?

"You're on our circle," the Core Couple man said. "I'm Pete. This is Lissette."

"Mario."

"And that's Loren and Teresa."

After the hellos, the atmosphere relaxed, Mario no longer felt invisible. Something brushed against his foot. He looked up at Loren and Teresa. They both smiled. Before the conversation continued, the gate to the pool deck opened and three other people entered and disrobed. It was another young man and two young women. They knew the Core Couple and Loren and Teresa.

"And here comes the rest of the crew!" Pete said.

Within moments, hugs and kisses and high fives went around amongst the now crowded tub. Mario already lost track of the others' names, yet he suddenly knew that wasn't as important as the level of intimacy amongst this group. It was true, he thought, they were all together. He knew where this was heading.

Soon after, the bathers began sipping hard seltzer from aluminum cans, passing around vape pens, and casually hanging off each other. Even Loren and Teresa. Pete passed Mario a seltzer. He declined, until Loren hit his knee against Mario's underwater and said, "Come on, we won't bite," followed by Teresa, who said, "Hard," after which Mario felt fingers—hers?—graze his thigh.

In college, Mario's friends called him Blackout. In their heyday, Mario was known to wake up on a couch in the Student Union building, in the backseat of a car, in someone's closet. The faster he drank, the sooner it came. Tonight, however, he knew one White Claw couldn't erase his memory, but how he got from the hot tub back to the Pete and Lisette's place was indeed a blur. Perhaps it was all the flirty talk and the brushing up of limbs against bodies and the second-hand smoke and how it all felt so exhilarating and natural that he would accept their offer to continue the party so close to home.

At one point, perhaps by his third White Claw, he woke his cell phone. No messages. 9:38 p.m. It seemed early. Rose was likely reading to the girls by now, plus, Mario was only a few driveways down from his home. It wasn't like he was out at a bar, yet, he decided to put his phone on airplane mode. He rarely did that, and when he did, life surged through him, a little attempt at reclaiming what he'd lost so long ago.

"Mario, right?" Teresa had sidled up to him. Hip-hop filled the living area mixing with the chaos of a muted animated show on the plasma screen. "It's insane we literally share the same street but we don't know each other." She exhaled after puffing her vape pen. "Are you…Mexican?" she went on. Loren had moved over to them.

"Yes, well, Mexican-American."

"Well, Lorenzo here is from Spain." Teresa inhaled again, then offered him her vape.

"Oh, no thank you, I—I don't smoke," Mario said, which was a lie. He had a sizable stash of buds and joints in the bottom drawer of his filing cabinet. "I mean, I don't vape. Spain, really?"

"Si," Loren said. "So, then you smoke?"

"Well, yeah, but…"

"But what?" Teresa said. "Mario, you need to relax, what's bugging you? Us?"

"No, I—"

"Come." Loren motioned Mario up the stairs off the kitchen. Teresa followed. Maybe the alcohol was kicking in, but time moved a bit faster, and soon Mario was puffing a pipe packed with marijuana from Loren, then passing it to Teresa. She coughed after her toke and Loren patted her back. She passed it back to him and gave him a little peck on the cheek.

"That's how they do it in Spain, right, Lorenzo?" Teresa laughed.

"That's right," Loren passed the pipe to Mario and leaned forward to offer a peck to Mario's cheek. Mario recoiled at first, then let the young man's cheek touch his, after which Mario pulled from the pipe, then, handed it to Teresa, whereupon she leaned forward offering her cheek. Mario hesitated, then reciprocated, and just as soon his lips went to her cheek, she turned to face him, their lips scraping awkwardly.

Teresa laughed and set the pipe down. "See, I told you we wouldn't bite!"

Loren smiled and laughed, nodding his head, and planted his hand on the back of Mario's robe, just above his swim trunks. The young man patted Mario there and let his hand drift downward just a bit.

"Oh, wow, I need to get home," Mario said, checking his phone.

"So soon?" Teresa pouted. She reminded him of Martha Stewart, whom he actually had a low-key crush on.

"No te vayas, tío," Loren said, puffing on the pipe.

"I have to get up—and then he remembered he was out of work.

"Maybe one more," he said pointing to the bedroom door, waking his phone, and switching it off airplane mode.

"Another drink?" Teresa said, pointing to her can of White Claw.

"But before that—" Loren said, passing the pipe back to Mario, mocking him with puckered lips.

"Ha, ha… tío," Mario said, accepting the pipe and faking a puff.

Back downstairs, the ambiance had shifted. The pairs had moved in on each other. The lights were lower. Netflix was playing but no one was watching amidst the fondling.

Pete stood up to meet the three.

"Another drink," he said, leading them to the fridge.

"Actually, I just need some water," Mario said.

"Okay, okay," Pete shrugged. "You two didn't scare him, did you?"

Teresa draped her arm around Loren's neck. "Nah, he's tired. Has to put the kids to bed." She winked.

Mario gulped his water. "Thank you, thank you," he said. "How often do you—" Mario waved his hand around the room.

"Netflix and chill?" Pete said. "Almost every night. Come over anytime. Come on, guys."

Pete took Teresa's hand, and she took Loren's.

"We'll be waiting," Teresa said, following Pete to the couch. On the coffee table sat more pipes and buds.

Loren cocked his chin at Mario.

"See you later, tío."

"Okay, goodnight, you guys," Mario said.

Teresa blew him a kiss.

Outside their door, under the night sky, his phone showed one text.

Goodnight

No emojis. No punctuation. Rose was furious.

The smell woke him the next morning. In the downstairs half bath, where they were toilet training the kitten, awaited a generous pile of diarrhea. This was day four of the cat's digestive woes. They had changed the food; however the food was only part of this cat's stress. Becca and Bella tormented it with their squeals of delight and how they tried to capture it anytime of day, plus, it was a rescue and had been neglected, so it had no desire to be loved. It only knew tough love, which meant hiding under the couch twenty-three out of the twenty-four hours of the day.

Rose had thought it would help the girls unglue themselves from their screens. It did not. If anything it had awakened Mario's dormant allergies and had turned him into the Head of Animal Husbandry. And, cleaning the rings of the cat toilet training contraption was nothing like scooping up clumps from a litter box. It meant scraping up the feces with a gloved hand and flushing them down the toilet, then washing the rings with a hose outside and bleaching them, then Lysol-ing the whole bathroom to eradicate the smell. And it meant sweeping up all the litter the cat had kicked up in the process. Thank god Mario didn't have to log in this morning because he was not in the mood.

Gail pinged him after he'd spent a good half hour on clean up.

Day 1 of "No Work Period" (sad face emoji)

Right?!, he replied, followed by, *but not missing District Check In* (laughing with tears emoji)

Mario parked himself in his usual corner of the galley kitchen setting out the cereal bowls, slicing bagels for the toaster, and whisking eggs. Why he kept making eggs every morning he didn't know. The girls only pushed them around the plate once they found out what they really were. Becca was fine with it until Bella continually reminded her it was an unborn baby chick that came from a bird butt. He'd set out the food and they'd eat and he'd shuttle them off to school and when he'd come home, Rose would still be asleep. She'd sometimes sleep until 10:45. They used to have midday sex, which was a good thing, and then that faded when the company started scheduling more calls to prepare for Transformation, which was around the time she enrolled in telepathy.

Back home after drop off, Mario sorted through the mail and papers on the "Catch-all counter" and found a few worksheets.

Cues as Clues: Verbal & Non-Verbal
Tapping In, Tapping Around
Perception is Reality
Interpretation vs. Translation
Eyes Don't Lie

Rose's notes showed she was into this thing, the page filled with sentences and bullet points and arrows. Then, not so into it, what with all the doodles. And then, a name. Phillip. It was written in a few places in different script. Cursive. Block letters. Mario didn't need to telepathy to decipher that she was in love with someone named Phillip. He used his own over-thinking brain for that.

They had never cheated on each other. At least they'd never admitted if they had. She travelled a lot for her party planning, which was only day trips for weddings and communions and bar mitzvahs, but she had lots of these short-term intense relationships with brides and grooms-to-be, fathers and mothers, and bachelors and bachelorettes. She'd made and stayed friends with many of them; had even become part of their lives.

He went to three-day trade shows and rah-rah sales meetings in Vegas and Phoenix. He had overnights in LA and San Francisco and Palm Springs. He had these "client-friends" pretty much all over the place. Women, men, business leaders, financial decision makers, mid-levels, and peons all of whom he took to dinners and bars and sky boxes, and who embraced him like their benefactor brother—the guy with a big heart and a corporate AmEx. And yeah, a lot of the ladies charmed him, would try to lace their fingers into his, nuzzle their noses into his neck. Some of the guys even doing what Loren did last night: testing the waters to see if maybe, just maybe.

Rose came downstairs dressed and ready, eyes a bit sunken.

"Morning," she said, looking down for her shoes.

"Morning," he said. "Coffee?"

"No. Gotta run."

"Class?"

"No. Waxing," she said, tying her shoes. "It's in the calendar."

She'd been getting waxed on the regular now for about a month.

"I can get the girls," he said.

"That'd be great," she said.

She grabbed her keys and that moment came, where they had to decide: come in for a hug or kiss or something. Anything?

And a miss. She was in a hurry. He was not.

"Let me know if you want to get lunch," he said.

"Umm, okay." The okay a surrogate for no. "Oh, thanks for cleaning the litter. Sorry I didn't get to that," Rose said.

"Yeah, it was more messed up this morning."

Then, Rose was off. The house felt eerily silent again.

He went back to her class papers, then to the internet to research the school. Under "About Us," the link to the staff only showed a list of names, no pictures. P. Carter was one of them.

Then, from under the couch emerged little Jasper, the rescued American Short Hair waiting for absolute calm to make his daily appearance. He was a cute little thing. A mostly orangish coat with hints of brown stripes, a kind of pitiful mini tiger. Mario smiled at him, called and psp-psp-psp'd to him as the cat walked by. Mario thought Jasper was on his way to the bowl to eat his morning meal, however it was headed for the half bath where Mario had not replaced the rings over the toilet, nor the litter. Jasper went in, but found the space unacceptable, so he turned back toward the living area, then lifted his backside to a squatted position and shat with great emphasis on the blue paisley rug.

"Fuck me," Mario said.

Mario wasn't a gym rat by any stretch, but now he had a routine, and was getting friendly with some of the regulars at the Ariana Clubhouse Gym, mostly the older men who came early in the morning hacking their coughs on the machines. Mario wondered what the other early birds had going on in their lives, especially the ladies who used the elliptical machines on the highest settings, their bodies moving aggressively slow. Or the young men who pumped in small quick movements with very little weight. Was it doing anything at all?

He ran his fob over the sensor to unlock the door when he saw Pete and Lisette inside. Even when they worked out they couldn't keep their hands off each other. Mario thought to turn around right there, and then he reminded himself that nothing happened last night—there was no reason to be ashamed. He was making new friends.

"Mario!" Pete called to him. "Hey!"

"Hey, you two, what's going on? Thanks for having me over last night."

"Definitely," Pete said, going back to a machine.

Lisette stood up from the mat she was on and smiled at Mario.

Mario stretched near them, trying not to look at Lissette's midriff.

"So, what do you do?" Pete said, pulling down on the lat machine. Mario looked up from his downward dog.

"I'm…in between jobs." He sprung to his feet. "Mine was actually recently eliminated."

"Oh, shit, I'm sorry man," Pete said.

"AI." Mario swung his arms, hugging himself.

"Oh," Pete said. "Yeah."

"And you?" Mario said. "What do you do?"

"AI." Pete finished another set.

"You're kidding me," Mario's shoulders slumped.

"No, seriously. I'm a product developer," Pete said.

"So am I," Lissette smiled, then bent forward to touch her toes. Mario averted his eyes.

He had a thousand questions. What was the actual work? How

long had they been doing that? Were they hiring? And yet, his mind went to how much fun they were having. How they had created some kind of life that involved tending to their carnal needs first, and how that was probably the best thing you could do for yourself. Self first, work last.

"I'm—wow, you'll have to tell me more about it. I'm so curious."

"Come over anytime," Lissette said. "We're watching movies again tomorrow night."

"Yeah, come by. Oh, and I think Teresa likes you," Pete said.

"Oh wow, I'm flattered. But, I'm married. With kids."

"Yeah, we've seen you around," Pete said. "What's your wife's name?"

"Rose."

Pete and Lissette looked at other, holding in laughs.

"What?" Mario said.

"Nothing, nothing." Pete stifled his giggles.

"It's just—we have this theory," Lissette said, "that women named after flowers are crazy.

"Lily, Daisy, Violet," Pete said.

"He dated a Zinnia once," Lissette laughed.

"I'm sorry, I didn't mean to—look, I don't even know your wife. Sorry," Pete said.

"No, no, it's fine. It's funny." Mario thought for a moment. *Was Rose crazy?*

"Hey, we were just finishing up here," Pete said. "And about coming over and stuff, we just hang out, you know. We're relaxed people. We don't judge. And I didn't meant to embarrass you about Teresa. She's a really nice lady."

"Yeah," Lissette said. "When you come over, you just leave your worries at the door."

"You're really cool people," Mario said.

"Come over and we'll talk AI. There's a lot going on with it. Oh, and sorry about your job."

"Thanks. It's okay," Mario said. "What time?"

"Late thirty." Pete winked.

Mario's prior mornings began with a check of his calendar to remind him what was ahead; whether he needed to shower or shave, put on a shirt, or stay off camera. When he had to leave the house to see customers in person, which came less and less leading up to his termination—a sign he had ignored to his peril—he relished in the preparation. There was a low-grade thrill in booking a Hilton, packing an overnight bag, and driving ninety to a two-hundred miles away. Once, when he had to go to Bakersfield for a meeting, he bought a pack of Marlboros for old-time's sake and smoked only one when he arrived, then threw the pack away in disgust.

But now it was the family calendar only, which was filled with little blocks of time fixed on the routines of their lives. Drop off and pick up times, doctor appointments, dental check-ups, beauty treatments, car maintenance, parties, and play dates. The AI would tell you when it was time to leave, and even if you weren't going there, it would remember you went there last week and give you a little nudge on the same day. Previously, he would add his blocks of work time so Rose knew when and where he was. He laughed a bit thinking she didn't need to know that anymore with her telepathy and the fact that he didn't have a job.

Today, she was out all day with several meetings preparing for a wedding. Tonight, she had Telepathy, plus, Thursdays were

Daddy-Daughter Date Nights, or 3DN, they called it. Bella dispensed her usual dramatics at drop off—the kid hadn't quite recovered from two years of quarantine once she realized that you didn't have to actually leave the house for anything. Pick up was uneventful except for the girls' desire to return home immediately to get back to their screens. Mario was past the point of caring about this. Rose had never seemed to care in the first place. She called the tablets a modern pacifier, and although he hated them, Mario couldn't disagree.

They'd fallen into a Chuck E. Cheese rut for 3DN, but Mario obliged. It was their haven before the pandemic, and had risen back to popularity in recent months, now that Rose let them touch the games again with infections down to a minimum. They only had a year at best of going to that place as the girls would soon age out of themed restaurants.

He texted Rose: *Do you want to meet us at CEC after your class?*

Rose was also the Queen of Leaving Mario on Read. Her usual refrain several hours later: *I just saw this.*

Once past the turnstile, the smell of Parmesan on the nose, Mario wanted to puke.

"What do you girls want?" he said

"Cheese," they said.

He didn't need to ask.

"Here, let's go get your cards filled," he said.

And they were off. He considered a beer but stuck with Coke. Scanning his phone, a wave of anxiety hit him. She was there learning to read minds with *him*. Someone named Phillip. Her location was on. Indeed she was there. And it was close, not one exit away from where they were. He could go, check in on them.

But how? They could leave early, swing by the neighborhood. He could take the girls home, ask Toni a few doors down to watch them. But that was only in emergencies. Or, he could leave them. They'd probably never notice. And then, he found his answer. Their neighbors from the other side of the complex, the Timkins. He had texted Randy earlier, told him they were going there, would they like to join. Like a miracle, they actually showed up. Mario waved at them, already planning out the excuse in his head. He and Randy were close. They drank beer together at the hot tub from time to time. The Timkins would for sure watch the girls. Mario would only need to run to the pharmacy to get some Pepto, that was it.

"Oh absolutely," Darcy said. "We'll keep an eye."

"Girls," Mario put a hand on Becca and Bella's shoulders. "Daddy's stomach is messed up. I need to run to the CVS. It'll take me only about 15 minutes. Just right over there. To get some Pepto. Ms. Darcy and Mr. Randy are going to keep an eye on you." He rubbed his belly.

"I wanna come," Becca said.

"Oh, I can watch Bella if Becca goes." Darcy nodded.

"Oh, no honey, just stay here with Ms. Darcy. It's kind of an emergency," Mario said.

"Come on, honey, let's go play with Seth and Ben." Darcy guided Becca away, mouthed, *go ahead*, to Mario. *Thank you* he mouthed back.

"Oh, their pizza's coming out soon. Can you grab it?"
Thumbs up.

Rose's car was not there, and her location finder was now off. He drove around the back of the building. Nothing. His calendar widget still showed "Rose: Telepathy. 2376 India Way." Did they get out early? He had heard somewhere that it only took twenty minutes to have an affair.

Back at Chuck E. Cheese, the kids were playing well. Darcy and Randy were drinking a beer with Rose. She had apparently decided to join them.

"You okay?" she said. "Did you get some Pepto?"

"Oh, yeah, stomach just felt awful," Mario said.

"It's this food," Darcy said, taking a bite of pizza.

"Yeah, but he didn't have any!" Rose said.

"How do you know?" Mario shot her a look.

"The girls told me."

"Oh." Mario sat.

"So, this telepathy class?" Darcy drained her beer. "I'm curious about it."

"I hear it's going to be one the skills AI can't do," Randy said.

"I doubt that," Mario said. "It's only a matter of time."

Rose shot back. "Well, anyway, it's fun and interesting. And I kind of think I'm opening my third eye."

"Do you think there will be third eye doctors?" Mario asked Randy.

"Hilarious, but I have no idea. I only do teeth."

"I should have picked a field like dentistry," Mario said

"He just lost his job." Rose leaned in.

"Oh, I'm sorry," Darcy said.

Randy reached over, patted Mario on the shoulder.

"It's okay," Mario said. "It was time. I need to reinvent."

"So, what's next?" Randy said.

"I don't." Mario said, turning to Rose. "You can see the future, can't you?"

Darcy went for her drink, but it was empty.

"Kids!" Randy shouted toward the arcade, none of either couples' offspring insight. "Time to go."

Back home, the Cold War continued.

"Are you on kids tonight?" Mario said, then immediately corrected with, "I mean, I'm going to get them to bed right now. I'd like to go to the hot tub again. Is that okay?"

"You don't have to ask me," she said. "You can do what you want."

"Are you okay?"

"Am I okay? Um, that comment at Chuck E. Cheese. It was kind of rude."

"About what?"

"About how I can read the future?"

"It was a joke."

"It didn't feel like a joke," she said. "It was how you said it."

"Look, please don't use your new tricks you're learning or whatever. It was just a joke."

"New tricks?"

"You're trying to read my mind, aren't you?" Mario said.

"No. I'm not. That's not how it works."

Silence. He felt looked into, not looked at.

"You know, you may want to avoid the hot tub," she said. "Especially if you had diarrhea. There's a sign there that says if you've had active diarrhea, you shouldn't get in."

"I didn't have diarrhea."

"The Pepto?" Rose said.

"Oh, it was gas. Bloating. I haven't been digesting well."

"Dad! Can I have a bath?" Bella shouted from upstairs.

"No, it's too late," he said.

"They need a bath. Especially after Chuck E. Cheese," Rose said

Mario froze. He was about to ask her about her telepathy instructor. But now was not the time. The Quadruple and friends were meeting soon. He'd have to get over there.

"Okay," he said. "Start the water."

After the girls were bathed, brushed, combed and lulled with stories, Mario slipped out.

Pete was wearing a Hawaiian shirt unbuttoned. Lissette was in a grass skirt with shells over her breasts.

"I didn't know it was Hawaiian night," Mario said.

"Neither did we," Pete said. "Come in. We just do stupid shit like this every now and then."

"Mario!" Teresa and Loren shouted from the couch. They stood to greet him with European cheek kisses, he in a floral print shirt and shorts, Teresa in her own skirt and tube top. He gave them their kisses and a brief, wild possibility wedged into his thoughts.

"You look like you need a drink," Teresa said.

"And a smoke," Loren said.

"Where's the rest of the crew?" Mario said.

"On the way," Lissette said, topping off cups with rum. Pete put a cup in Mario's hand. "Here," he said, "Catch up."

Rum and Mario did not mix well. It made his throat itch, but tonight, he thought nothing of it. The liquor went down easy and warmed his insides. The vapes came around, and on the TV was a reality singles show in a faraway paradise, where the main feature was the skin of gorgeous bodies. With the sound low, drown out by an ambient electronic beat Pete had selected from his playlists, everything went glazy, Mario himself swimming in a forbidden ether. He found himself comfortably wedged between Teresa and a new party guest, a young lady whose name he'd quickly misplaced. Loren sat at Mario's feet, watching the show, resting his back on Mario's legs.

When the clothes started to come off, Mario knew it was too late. He'd already made up his mind before he came, like the song said, the rap jam he listened to in the gym to feel dangerous and sexy. WAP, WAP, WAP, Megan Thee Stallion rapped as he grunted with dumbbells.

"Just relax," Teresa said. "It's best to just keep your eyes closed until you're ready to open them."

Hands against skin, reaching all over, up, under, around, some parts firm, other parts soft, moisture of sweat and saliva, fluids. It built around him like a bubble of heat and sin, it grew and thickened viscous on his flesh the more he let go, the more he let himself get lost in the experience. There were no borders, no customs, nothing to declare. It went on forever and also lasted only moments. He didn't remember what touched what or what went where. It was like those times he had blacked out, yet in place of a hangover was a distinct electricity coursing his skin under the sweat and essences of their bodies, like sweet and pungent chemical traces, leaving an indelible mark on his psyche.

After, he skipped the cigarettes. He jumped in the shower with Teresa and Loren. He'd never been that close to two people naked at the same time. Maybe in college in the dorm showers, but it was always such a hurried thing. Mario had never been this relaxed in his entire life

"I have to ask," he said. "Why do you stroll your dog around like that?"

Soaping herself, her back toward him, Teresa turned to face him. "He has arthritis, you asshole."

Loren gave Mario a look of consolation, tilted his head for Mario to get out of the shower.

"Sorry," Mario said, and this moment of clarity zapped him out of his ecstatic haze. He quickly dried off, dressed, and found his phone downstairs where he had left if before the orgy. Six texts. Two missed calls.

Bella threw up. Where did you put that Pepto?
Hello, are you still at hot tub?
When are you coming home?
Where are you?
Are you at a neighbor's house????
???

"Holy fuck," he said. "I have to go."
"Bye," Loren said.
"I'm sorry. About that comment," Mario said to Teresa.
"It's fine," she said. "Everything okay."
"Ah, no," Mario said.
"Location finder on?" Teresa stepped out of the shower.
"What? Yes. How did you know?"
"You're a terrible liar," she said, then blew him a kiss.

Outside, dressed but hair still damp, he rushed home. Rose intercepted him halfway under a street lamp.

"Where in the hell were you? Who's place did you just come from? Are you wet?"

"I was at the hot tub. I stopped by these neighbors' place after. They were at the hot tub, too. Is Bella okay?"

"What? Neighbors? She's fine. I put her back to bed," Rose said.

"Sorry. I just got distracted."

They walked back to their house. Rose stayed silent, then began prognosticating.

"You weren't at the hot tub. And you never went to CVS."

"Here you go again," he said. "Trying to read my mind."

"No. I checked your location. I've seen those kids down there. That young, sexy couple. I know what they're up to. You don't need telepathy to know they're swingers. And, I checked the bank. No CVS purchases. I had a hunch."

"I left Chuck E. Cheese to go see where you were. Your location was off."

"You were spying on me?" Rose said.

"Who the fuck is Phillip?" Mario said.
Rose stopped walking. They stood in the driveway, the front door ajar. She pursed her lips.

"I saw your notes, saw the name scribbled all over. Are you in love with your instructor or something?"

"Let's go inside to talk about this," she said.

"Are you fucking him?" he said.

"Let's go inside," she pointed. The door moved just slightly.

"Tell me." Mario demanded.

"No." She crossed her arms. Huffed. "Phillip…is a friend."

"What kind of friend?"

She pulled out her phone, tapped the screen. Blue light bathed her face. She turned the screen toward Mario. A handsome man's face stared back, waiting for input. His idle face, so very humanlike, perked up. His expression changed.

"Rose?" the man's voice said. "Is that you, babe?"

Rose turned the phone back to herself, tried to silence it.

"Just a minute," she said to the screen.

"Who the fuck is that? Is that…a bot?"

"It's a friend. I told you," she said.

"You're talking to a fucking robot."

Their front door opened more. A silhouette appeared, a small animal. A cat. Jasper sauntered outside. He stepped gingerly at first, sniffing the lilies and hyacinths in the flower bed with curiosity.

"Jasper, no!" Rose shouted, trying to approach the cat.

Mario ran toward Jasper, but it darted the opposite way.

"Don't scare it!" Rose said.

Just then, Jasper turned in the other direction. Mario was within reach. He lunged, but fell to his knees. Jasper took off into a sprint, bounding toward a hedge. They both followed it trying to keep up with it, but after a while, the cat was gone. They stopped running. Rose leaned forward, hands resting on her knees to catch her breath. Mario paced in a small circle, hands on top of his head.

"Fuck," he said.

Teresa, still freshly showered, walked by, nodded hello.

"Everything okay?" she said.

"Yeah. No. Hi," Rose said. "Our cat just go out."

"Oh no." Teresa covered her mouth. "What's he look like?"

"Like a little tiger," Mario said.

Teresa tutted. "I'll keep an eye out for him. When I walk my dog."

"Thank you." Rose said eyeing Teresa as she walked off. "Goodnight."

Mario and Rose turned back to head home, but she stopped and faced him, reached for his head, felt his hair. She rubbed some of his wet strands in her fingers, her eyes boring into his with deep inquiry. He glanced at her hand, still clutching her phone. Phillip called to her. She looked down at it, shoved the phone in her pocket. She faced Mario. He felt something he hadn't felt from her but maybe a few times in his life. One was at the altar, when they had exchanged vows. The other times were when they shared exhausted looks at the births of their girls. This look was like those, but different. It was raw and intense and all-knowing, but what came back to him revealed something else entirely. They didn't need to say anything else to each other. They both knew. They both knew they were well past the beginning of the end.

LIVED EXPERIENCE

Outer Caribbean Sea, 1862

The air, dense with the scents of urine and vomit, burned through the cloth James held over his nose. He'd kept his own stomach acid down this long—unlike the other stowaways who couldn't stop expelling as the ship rocked side to side in the dark. He'd never been one to have a gag reflex, but he had been on the verge of having a mishap in his pants for several hours. He was afraid that, should he unclench his buttocks, it would all come blasting out. It had happened before. Many times. The Tyler's were notorious for their loose bowels. That, plus the sardines he'd been eating the past two weeks, given to him by his sister, Sarah, certainly had not helped.

James could not crouch due to the uncomfortable pressure, so he moved upright dancing a nervous jig, switching between holding the cloth over his nose and mouth and clutching a railing inside the small utility hatch, where he and five other men had been shoved into upon leaving Liverpool.

"Who are you dancing with over there, Tyler, and with that cloth over your face? Never smelled piss before?" one of the seated stowaways spat toward James. The young man, sweaty and pale, his eyes rolling in his head with queasiness.

"Fine. I'm fine. I need to—find…a…" James looked around in desperation. He could not hold it much longer.

"The water closet?" the young man laughed. "You're in it."

James turned to the hatch door, yanking and jiggling the knob to open it, but James recalled, just as the young man turned to him once more and said, "We're locked in, remember? They only come once a day to let us out," followed by a stream of vomit coming from his mouth.

"I can't hold it!" James screamed and let go: of the door handle, of the knot in his stomach, of the clench of his sphincter. He squatted, wincing in pain and relief, shrieking all the while, both comforted and embarrassed. The other men howled in disgust with James' addition to the competing aromas prompting a few of them to wretch once more. The ship pitched hard to the right, then left, sending the young men to one side of the small space, then the next. They toppled onto and over each other, each roll of the boat mixing their fluids and odors.

One young man sprung to his feet in a frenzy, arms and legs windmilling to the door. He grabbed and yanked the knob, pulling and screaming. He pushed his shoulder into it, breaking it open. The others stood, rushing to the open hatch, but they were met with a wall of water cascading into the small walkway outside the door. What was once a hidden spot a couple of levels below deck had become exposed by a gash in the starboard side just above them. Torrents poured in, dousing them and their smells. The men screamed, pulling at each other, grasping at anything they could.

"I don't know how to swim!" one yelled.

"Neither do I!"

"Hold on!"

The ship rolled again, and they were all tossed to the opposite corner. The water, now at their shins rose higher by the second. They scrambled to the open door, fighting to get out.

"Abandon ship! Abandon ship!" A voice from above bellowed.

"Find a dingy, lads!" Someone yelled.

James ran as best he could down the dark, wet gangway, the others pushing around him. New faces, other shipmates and crew, were coming their way holding buckets and banging them on the walls yelling abandon ship. James tripped and fell, his face submerged in the wet muck. Feet, knees, hands gouged into his backside. A stampede moved over him, no one reaching for him. Each time he tried to lift his head, he gasped for air and screamed for help. The boat pitched again, the rolling of the hull more intense than ever.

"Help!" he cried, trying to lift himself out of the rising water, feet and elbows and knees still knocking into him.

"Help!" he screamed, then fell again, his shoulders now under the water, bubbles washing over him, the darkness turning now to pitch blackness.

Near Future

Matt pulled his headset off. This was the third time this scene had played, and it was the only time he'd watched it until the end. He hadn't made it through the two first times thinking something was wrong, that this was a malfunction, perhaps an incorrect file sent to his account. But the name was indeed James Tyler. His great-great-great grandfather. He put the headset on one more time, fast-forwarded to James' face in the water, but then nothing again. Blackness. He knew James was likely a stowaway, but he never knew exactly what happened. Did the ship sink? Did he actually survive? He had to have survived, otherwise, Matt would not be on this planet.

Matt opened the LivedExperience app. It offered no pointers. Only kitschy how-tos of other users watching their ancestors lives play out before their eyes; courageous men and women on horseback or around campfires or on wagon trains. LivedExperience touted their blend of their vast DNA repository, their access to historical records and documents, plus, the wonder of artificial intelligence, which brought forth a "veritable movie—a lived experience of your ancestors lives."

He pinged their customer support chat.

…

How may I help you today?

Was this a scene? A clip? The start of the movie? Matt tapped his chin.

Are you still there?

He typed: My movie abruptly ends after two minutes or so. It won't go past this one scene

Sorry to hear you have having this issue. Have you tried logging out and logging back in?

Yes.

Have you tried to power down the VR headset and power on again?

Yes.

Hmm…please standby by while we perform a remote reset to your system. This should only take a few moments!

While he waited, Matt picked up the headset and peeked in, not expecting to see anything, however the screen appeared to glitch showing snow and lines, then SMPTE color bars, followed by a quick series of new images. They flashed by so quickly, he could not make sense of them, but he perceived a stampede of horses, a hazy scene of a what appeared to be a barren desert, then a brief snippet of all-out war. He put the headset down.

Thank you for your patience! We have completed a restart of your system, which should generate the appropriate content. Please restart your segment and then let us know if there are any other issues.

Ok.

Is there anything else that I can assist you with at this time?

No. Thank you.

He always debated thanking them.

Thank you!

According to cousin Bruce, the self-proclaimed family historian, James Tyler was probably a criminal and needed to get out of England. He stowed away on a Trans-Atlantic cargo ship bound for the West Indies, St. Thomas perhaps, then somehow found his way to the mainland United States, which was in the throes of the Civil War. To gain citizenship, he pledged to support the Union Army at some point of entry, found his way to the Colorado Territory, where he enlisted in the Third Colorado Cavalry. After the war, James had found a Native American wife, relocated to New Mexico, and settled into a life of ranching. Bruce had buried himself in genealogy during the first waves of the virus because he had heard somewhere it was a proven way to fight porn addiction, the clicking and searching and hunt for more somehow a surrogate for the dopamine rush of explicit content. Matt never asked, but Bruce offered more than needed, as always, and the family benefited because they at least knew a bit more than stories handed down through the generations.

Bruce had added to the family folklore at last with some facts, which further fomented the idea that the Tyler's were the descendants of a would-be John Smith-meets-Pocahontas love story; that Matt and Bruce and all their cousins were a blend of two fine races, one of which Bruce was sleuthing daily to confirm their purported Native American origins, so that they might, as Bruce envisioned, take advantage of benefits from the guilty pockets of Uncle Sam.

But Matt was skeptical. He never believed in the stories. He never quite felt English or Native American. And if their great-great-great grandfather was a crook, what was his crime? Were they all not descendants of lawbreakers, bound to repeat the cycle? Plus, he only considered himself half—if that—of the gringo side of the family. He relished in his mother's side, Mexicans with a nice clean ancestral line to Mexico City. No thieves, no marauders.

Matt was going to find out on his own. He'd submitted everything LivedExperience asked for. He'd even shared the files Bruce had kept that were not found in the government archives: actual post-war pensions, book clippings in microfiche, a purported colorized daguerreotype of the man himself.

Matt placed the headset over his eyes. He laid back on the couch, raised his hand and tapped the start button floating above him. The first frame was darkness, just how the boat scene started, for which Matt almost ripped the headset off, however in place of the tumult of a rolling sea and groans from the stowaways, low voices emerged from what appeared to be a deep purple sky, stars still twinkling, but with the threat of morning sun not far away.

The predawn light cast shadows on the faces of a few young but gaunt men, creases of worry and concern etched around their eyes and mouths. The flick of a match to light crude tobacco cigarettes amongst them illuminated the fear in their eyes, the bright red a temporary uniting spark.

"We take out the warriors. Only the warriors," a man called Mariano said. He translated into Spanish to a few of the other men. "Solo los guerreros."

"And you, Santiago," Mariano said, clutching the white man's shoulder, the grasp of a friend, "you will steal their horses."

The VR simulation zoomed onto the man called Santiago. Matt recognized him. He was James from the seasickness scene. He was James Tyler, his great-great-great grandfather. The supposed Civil War soldier.

"But what of the other companies. They are going to follow Chivington's orders. Eradicate all of them," Santiago said.

"We are not going to worry about them. We are following the mission. Kill Black Kettle, the chiefs, and the men." Mariano exhaled smoke, surveying the horizon. The Sand Creek was just beyond the small plateau where they stood hiding in darkness, surrounded by horses and the other companies of the Cavalry. They were a huge force, a sprawling army of over six hundred men, yet all of the smaller groups seemed to be on their own islands, having their own hushed conversations. In moments, they would mount and ride. At dawn's first light, the bugle would sound and they would attack.

"Mount up," Mariano said.

The view panned wide as the companies mounted their horses, legs slung over saddles, boots settling into stir-ups, the collective clang of spurs jolting the beasts of burden, men hushing the whinnying. It played like a somber choreography, as though these events had happened over and over, rehearsed to perfection, but what Matt knew of these men, as relayed to him by historian Bruce, was that *all* of them were crooks and convicts; the entire group was a ragtag of broken young men recruited to a war machine whose side project was genocide. Just then, the scene froze, and a boxed warning message appeared on screen: *The following scenes contain violent and distressing images. Viewer discretion is advised. Do you wish to continue?*

The words pulsed, waiting for Matt's response. He'd been sharing this new ancestry curiosity with his fiancé, Katie. She didn't think much of it, in fact she had warned him, saying he should be careful looking toward the past. You might not like what you find, she had said. Throughout the course of their relationship, they'd talked about their backgrounds and who their families were, and Katie had typically brushed off her otherwise standard Northern European lineage. She'd professed time and again that she was simply *American*. Whenever Matt asked what she thought about the Native Americans that once inhabited all the lands known as America, she'd shrug and say, "That was a long time ago."

Matt tapped the boxed warning and the scene continued. A bugle popped the silence of the still, misty morning, now bathed in dawn's first light. Like an aggressive rooster, the bugle signaled that the new day had arrived whether you liked it or not. The Cavalry moved forward fast, first in formation of a wide phalanx. Then, the companies fell in after each other forming a moving arrow of horse-mounted uniformed men heading straight for a Cheyenne encampment. Small puffs of smoke escaped from some of the tops of the teepees, that were assembled near a meandering shallow creek. The perspective suddenly went cinematic—the view now high above the rapidly closing distance between the front of the Cavalry and the village. Like a bird of prey, the perspective made a steep dive, speeding toward the tops of the teepees. Atop a pole of a larger teepee flew a small American flag along with a white flag. The view then shifted now to face the onslaught of the soldiers. They rushed headlong into the village, a tidal wave of stamping horses' hooves, gun smoke, and the guttural war cries of men simply acting on orders. Zooming into the scene, the frame went hazy with fog and smoke, and from the gray emerged the screams of women and the cries of children, the Cheyenne men yipping and calling back, their voices pitched and urgent as they assembled in a frenzy to defend their village. Swords slashing, guns blasting, arrows flying, smoke and tears, flashes of blood, more screams, more agony—all of it blended together into a horrific symphony, the only soundtrack to this film—to this moment in time.

Matt paused it. He couldn't stomach any more. He fast-forwarded and the gruesome battle continued, but it wasn't a battle. The Cavalry were not fighting anyone insomuch as they were eradicating humans. He fast-forwarded for what seemed like minutes with his eyes closed, the scenes becoming even more brutal and terrifying, when he did have the strength to peek. Then, the view shifted to Mariano and James, called Santiago, and the men in their company from the early morning scene. Mariano was shouting in Spanish, then he turned to James and said in English, "Santiago, let's go, let's go now, to the corral."

The Cavalry men of Mexican origin stayed behind, held their line and did not draw their weapons. There were other companies that did the same through all this, that stood motionless in shock of the inhumanity they were watching unfold. Some backed away, some stayed solid, all did nothing. Meanwhile, Mariano and James, rode away from the massacre toward the back end of the village where a corral of horses stood. James fell behind Mariano, who had rushed ahead, and just then, a Cheyenne brave had stepped out from behind a nearby teepee. The warrior pulled his arrow back in his bow and aimed for James.

"Shoot!" Mariano shouted to James. "Shoot him!"

James dropped his right hand to reach for his pistol, but he froze, and then the view went pitch black, the echo of Mariano shouting "shoot" faded away, along with all the clatter and screaming filling the air. Matt was transported back to the previous scene he had thought was a glitch: the rolling ship, the seasick stowaways, James on the verge of a major accident. The scene played once again, each frame now etched in Matt's head. He tried to fast forward, but the controls didn't respond. The scene was beginning to make Matt nauseous. He was about to yank off the headset, but instead he closed his eyes and tried to breath and count to calm himself.

For a moment, he felt as though he was James himself, seasick and dizzy, bowels pinched up, buttocks locked tight. The breathing helped until the sound of James' gurgling face down in the brackish water returned. With that, Matt opened his eyes and gagged, fighting the bile coming up his own throat. Mariano's shouting returned, snapping Matt back to the previous scene, the point of view now fixed on James breathing heavily, unable to move his hands. He reached down, then put his hands up. The Cheyenne warrior issued a high-pitched cry, then let his arrow fly straight toward James. James shifted to the left to dodge it, the arrowhead piercing the sleeve of his raised arm. The point had cut the jacket fabric clean open, slicing the skin of James' left tricep. He felt it with his glove, a pool of blood staining the yellow leather.

"Run!" Mariano shouted.

The view shifted again, panning wide, showing James in a panic, his face and body the same way it looked in the stowaway locker: sick and no longer able to hold it. Zooming in on his face, James had let his bowels go one more time, now mounted in uniform. He held his stomach, buckling forward, unable to move his horse. The warrior meanwhile re-knocked his bow, and shot again. James ducked and squirmed in the saddle, kicking the horse to move forward. Finally, he was back at a gallop.

He caught up with Mariano, who was already at work opening the corral.

"What happened to you?" Mariano shouted over the whinnying of the horses.

"I made a mess," James said. "In my pants."

"Again?" Mariano said, lassoing a stallion. "Now, get to work."

The view panned wide, Mariano and James now miniature figures stealing horses, and running them away from the chaos of the massacre. The sun, now out but hidden by a patchwork of graying clouds, shone down on the aftermath below: a grisly scene of death, blood, a population ravaged to nothing. Matt wanted to see no more. He pulled off the headset, turned it off, and set it aside.

A few days later, Matt called his cousin Bruce. Matt needed answers.

"So, were not going to tell me that James Tyler was not only crook, but a war criminal?" Matt said.

"He didn't kill anyone," Bruce said.

"But he was there. And he stole their horses. And how do you know he didn't kill anyone?"

"He was doing his job," Bruce said. "You seem pretty messed up about it."

"It's awful. It's one of the most violent, bloody things I've ever seen. It was worse than *Full Metal Jacket*."

"You're always the exaggerator," Bruce said.

"Do you want to see it yourself?" Matt said.

"Not interested. Researching it was enough."

"It helped you, right?" Matt said. "With the porn?"

"Anyway, I'm glad you found out on your own," Bruce said. "That's why our great aunts and uncles never talk about him. They're ashamed."

"They should be," Matt said. "And he went by Santiago? Why was that?"

"Oh, yeah. I saw that one some records. Santiago is Spanish for James. Maybe he was just trying to fit in. Or doing some code switching identity crisis thing. We all do it."

Matt had no words. His cousin was explaining everything away. Making the atrocities acceptable.

"But remember—," Bruce started.

"I know what you're going to say," Matt interrupted. "It's all in the past, right? It's the same thing Katie says."

"See, she gets it," Bruce said. "You have to let it go. The past is the past. What he did doesn't make you who you are today."

"Well, it explains why all the Tyler's have messed up bowels," Matt said.

"James couldn't hold it. Twice."

"Oh my god, are you serious?" Bruce laughed. "I'd watch it just for that. How long is the code good for?"

"I don't know. A day? I don't think I can send it."

"Hey, just do a screen record, on the VR and send it to me," Bruce said.

"It's long," Matt said.

"Just try."

"All right. I'll let you know," Matt said.

He'd avoided it for a few hours. Katie had come home and he told her about. He offered to show her, but she smiled and said no, she wasn't interested. So, they weren't interested in looking at wounds and scars. They didn't want to face it. Who would anyway, when everything in this present time was so perfect and unblemished? Why would anyone want to bear witness to such tragedy?

Later that night, Matt turned on the VR once more. He opened the LivedExperience app and cued up the file. The duration was shorter. It seemed to have changed from the hour or so to about thirty minutes. He hesitated, his virtual hand pointing at the play button, but refusing to click. Maybe it reverted back to the stowaway scene; the flashback etched in James' memory, the origin story of the family's intergenerational trauma. He clicked play.

What unfolded in front of his eyes, wasn't the shipwreck. Nor was it the sweeping views of a cavalry about to attack. It was those scenes he couldn't watch earlier. The ones that had forced him to keep his eyes shut tight. Each movement played out in painful, slow detail, the video player somehow in a frame-by-frame speed. The gruesome actions did not let up, and every time he tried to close his eyes, the video stopped. When he opened his eyes, it resumed. His only recourse was to pull the headset off, but something stopped him. A call from the ghosts perhaps, a dormant gasp from other ancestors, or his own conscience made him—he stuck with it. He kept his eyes open and watched. He breathed through it, prayed, which he never did, and apologized. He would do it when they wouldn't. He would do it. He had to do it.

WARPATH

The sun had set. It was a beautiful night in that netherworld between Christmas and New Year's, when the air was both cool and crisp, but where the rays of the now disappeared sun had left a trace of buttery warmth. Pedro believed that one day, in the not-so-distant future, the holidays would evolve into a mandatory period of rest. That, in place of the rush to decorate and buy gifts and send cards and attend parties and cook and eat and watch TV and go to movies, that eventually everybody would give all that up, and instead go to spas and health clubs, soak in Jacuzzis, receive massages, meditate in the forest or on the beach. Medidate in the forest or on the beach being the most important of all. The world needed a dedicated resting period minus the commercialism. *How amazing would that be?* He would bring it up at the next meeting of the Benevolent Order of Woodland Creatures. The BOWC, of which he was acting secretary.

Besides, his children had lost the wonder of the season all together years before. On Christmas morning, instead of going downstairs to look at the presents delivered by Santa, they simply opened up their devices, logged in and began playing like it was just a regular morning. There was really nothing left for them to do but interact with whatever was on their screen at any given moment. They didn't even like toys anymore. They found that anything that required manipulation with the hands, or coordination with the eyes, was for babies. And they spoke differently. They used short sentences where the words were abbreviated, in a somewhat staccato beat, to describe how they were feeling or what they wanted. Their words were a series of acronyms and words that sounded like words. It was all quite confusing for Pedro, who thought he was very tuned into the world; however, the world he was tuned into was very different from theirs.

With his wool poncho on his back, walking stick in hand, and shoulder satchel across his chest, Pedro set out. Before he closed the front door, he looked back at the boys.

"Are you sure you don't want to come?" he said.

Their silence was his answer.

"Okay, well, I'll see you out there. Right?" He waited. "Right?"

Axel, the eldest, at last lifted his head up to his father.

"Bet," Axel said.

"I'll see you out there, right, Orion?" Pedro said. "Orion?"

But Orion was locked in, his eyes glazed over, his face expressionless.

"Orion?"

"Yeah, Dad," Orion said, eyes still focused on the screen on his lap.

Once down their street, Pedro turned right at the service cul-de-sac that met the mouth of the canyon. He headed down the trail that, during the pandemic, he and his boys had begun to clear, moving rocks and old branches, when the boys were only six and four-years-old. In those dreary days, they made big plans. They were going to make signs and arrows and a bench, maybe even build a little snack pantry where hikers could take a bottle of water or a granola bar before setting off into Rufina Canyon. The kids were so creative back then.

Pedro arrived at the midway point in no time. At the palm tree grove, he inhaled, looked up at the sky. Venus twinkled in the east. His ancient ancestors thought Venus was Quetzalcoatl, the feathered serpent. He used to tell the boys about that legend, about the pantheon of deities revered by the Mexica, which they loved at first, but found no interest in once the screens came.

He sat on a tree stump, pulled his satchel to his chest, unzipped it. He bit his lip looking at the black screen of his tablet. *Wasn't this just enabling their behavior?* No. It was meeting them where they are. That's the distinction he had made in therapy. Lean into it. Dance with it. Don't fight it. He tapped the black screen. It glowed back at him. That was the only way he was going to communicate with his sons that evening. He hit the Warpath app and his avatar, called Fire Starter, appeared on screen. He waited for the boys' avatars to appear.

He sent a few messages.

I'm here

I'm ready

Hello?

The boys were obviously doing something else on their devices. Perhaps playing another game, fiddling with another app, messaging with their cousins in Arizona, or simply making Pedro wait. He believed it was the latter, because that's what kids did, they found your weakness and exploited it to their benefit. They'd done this before. He'd storm back to the house and scold them, leaving them worse than when they started. They knew how sensitive he was about these fucking devices, and these fucking games, and so they would make him wait.

He scrolled, considered closing the app, but then the boys appeared. The tone of two dings announced their arrival. Storm Cloud and River Water. All the names were nature oriented. He stood, ready to play. He waited for their avatars to go holographic.

He was used to this part, too. They had also figured out they didn't have to go holographic. They could simply remain two-dimensional and play within the app. Going holographic meant a little more work, even at home. They'd have to at least stand, have their face, and preferably their bodies, at an angle for their devices to scan them, then broadcast them out to Pedro's device. Axel's hologram rendered.

"Hey buddy," Pedro said. "Is Orion coming?" Orion's two-dimensional avatar stood motionless.

"Orion! Come on. Dad's waiting," Axel said. "Hold on."

How these moments—waiting for technology to cooperate, or for humans to decide to interact with technology, went on forever. Behind every tap and stroke and click, there was always a human, and that human had prerogative. *Didn't they?*

"What's going on?" Pedro said.

"He's pooping," Axel said.

"Oh." Pedro sat back down on the palm tree stump. "Okay then, do you want to ping me when he's done?"

"Yeah," Axel said.

"Make sure you guys both—" Pedro started, but Axel's hologram disappeared.

Pedro pushed his diaphragm out while pulling in the crisp and loamy air of the canyon into his nostrils and down into his lungs. Exhaling, he closed his eyes and moved his hips in circles, then swayed his shoulders in an infinity eight pattern. *Breathe through, be true.* One of the BOWC's axioms. It was at this time of night when the coyotes came out. The mountain cats. He'd never seen an actual bobcat. They didn't come this close to town. But the coyotes, yes. He saw a pair two years ago, driving with the boys in the backseat. They stopped to look at them just standing there at the mouth of the canyon. The kids were fascinated.

Pedro knew the boys weren't coming. There would be no Warpath tonight. There would be no Warpath, likely not ever again. They were wise to it. They had figured it out. They had played as a family a grand total of four times. *Four times.* Pedro had so much hope for it. He shook his whole body to dispel the bad energy, then shut the tablet, shoved it in his bag and walked toward the mouth of the canyon.

He fished his mobile from his pocket, woke it, and went to Telegram to look for new messages. There were four, all voice texts. BOWC's went through cycles. Sometimes it was a flurry of video messages, then voice messages, voice messages, then video messages. The messages were always the same: dispatches from nature. Chirps and howls and screeches from the wild.

Hey fam, I'm here on a glorious hike around Chollas Lake!

You guys have to check out this new trail over at Kate Sessions Park. I can't believe I've never walked this! I mean, it's probably been here all along, but it's been overgrown.

It's a shame no one uses these canoes here at Mission Bay. They're just like, gathering dust and cobwebs!

Anyone want to meet tomorrow for a hike in Bonsall?

They were all pleas describing their collective plight: we're the only people that care about nature anymore. Get outside! Do something. The thread was designed for accountability to stay dedicated to being in nature, but it was more of a group therapy line. And there was always that moment when someone was removed from the group. When someone likely had had enough of the banter—or pressure—and had eventually found their way back indoors to some other occupation with technology. Or, they *went native.*

There were a few folks online, and he was feeling calm after his Energetic Expansion Exercises, but also perturbed because the boys were standing him up, and so he decided to record a video message instead of voice.

"Hey, everyone," he said, sighing with a smile. "It's the day before New Year's Eve—I guess, New Year's Eve Eve—and I'm here in Ruffin Canyon…my God, it's beautiful, but I'm a little bummed because I came out here to play Warpath with my kids, but they…stood me up. Again. And well, now I'm out here alone, and you know what? I don't mind it. It's beautiful and it's tranquil and…

His words trailed off. He turned his head away from the camera. His eyes suddenly stung and he felt his throat tighten up, his chin quivering. He spoke again, his voice caving, using his other hand to wipe his weeping eyes.

"I don't know, it's just…my kids, you know. They're so…addicted. They're hooked. They don't do anything else. I don't even know them. I'm only happy out here. I only want to be outside."

He paused. Wiped his eyes again. Looked into the camera.

"I'm thinking about going native."

He exhaled.

"Sorry, guys, just needed to get that off my chest. I don't know yet. Maybe. Just…send your thoughts. Whatever. Peace out for now."

Zeke and Stacey were the most recent to go native. It was better that they were a couple, everyone thought. Couples usually did better going native. The ones who went solo, well, no one really knew because they were never heard from again. Whereas, couples had networks of people who kept their memories alive. But the solo people, they just disappeared. That's how it worked.

You left society. You fell off the grid and never climbed back on. Someone said they had heard Zeke and Stacey were living outside Desert Hot Springs in a commune. A lot of people were flocking there. More solar energy.

On his walk back to the mouth of the canyon, Pedro replayed in his mind what he had just said. *Am I really thinking about going native?* He had entertained it once in a while, but there, a few minutes ago, was he for real? Or was it a call for help? Or maybe both? *Where would I actually go? What would the boys do without me?* He knew what they would do. They would go on playing their games and continue to order food and live life the way they were already living life. They were twelve and fourteen, and they were more equipped than ever. They would learn to live without a father the way they had learned to live without a mother. They would be, in short, fine.

"Yeah," he muttered. "They'll be fine."

Just before he stepped from the old river stone path they had forged during the pandemic to the pavement of the service cul-de-sac, he stopped and pulled his tablet out of his satchel. He logged into Warpath and he found exactly what he thought he'd find: no other players. Once back home, he found them where he knew he'd find them: still in front of their screens. He had no words for them. He set his satchel and walking stick down, took off the poncho, kicked off his shoes and walked past the boys.

"Dad?" Axel said. "Sorry. We're sorry we—"

Pedro didn't even turn to look at them as he walked upstairs to go take a cold shower.

The rules to Warpath were simple. All you had to do was walk and follow clues along the set path. You collected points when you identified and collected something in nature. Something real that you could add to your Nature Wallet. The app would scan the object and add it in. The game was designed for heavy users of video games, who were clocking more than ten hours a day of screen time a day, according to experts. Fucking experts. Warpath encouraged these children to get up and out of the house and simply walk. Pedro was convinced this would help him in his struggle to get his children to be more active.

It worked for a while, until, of course, the boys figured out how to manipulate the game. Once they had figured out all the clues and objects, the game lost its novelty. The first time, they had fun. Pedro added a hide-and-go-seek element to it and went far ahead, deep into the canyon, so that the boys wouldn't find him. Their holograms would meet at a neutral spot where they would make their plan: Pedro was to continue on and look for five clues, while Axel was to go another direction and look for three clues, and Orion, who disliked being outdoors, was to find one clue. After they found the clues, the boys would use the GPS to go to where Perdo was, and then they would all debrief and go back home. It would be about a two-mile walk. But once they scattered, the rules of the game revealed themselves to be of no challenge for neither father nor sons.

Pedro had read several reviews that said once heavy users were exposed to the natural elements, they would simply want to experience them. That the fresh air and sunshine would be too distracting, and thus the children would put their devices away. That was the pure simplicity of Warpath. The inventor of the game, Helix Toys, had said that children simply needed to be outdoors once again in order to reconnect with nature, and forget the beguiling lure of technology. After a while, it came out that the game was nothing more than a sham, a failed app, that only led to more advertisements. This was sort of funny in the beginning, when the boys began seeing countless ads for Ozempic and other diabetes medications, and sang along to the jingles, but very quickly it bothered Axel since he was now taking the pediatric indication of the blockbuster med for his Type II.

And the name, Warpath. It misleads the masses, especially the virtual gun crazy youth, who thought it was a battle game. There was also the cultural appropriation—that the idea of a warpath itself was one more blatant steal from indigenous heritage.

Regardless, Pedro wanted to play the game at least once a day with the boys, hoping it would return them to the world they so desperately needed to be part of. But tonight proved it was pointless. After his shower, he shouted from the balcony to go ahead and order their dinner—he wasn't hungry—and that they had to put themselves to bed.

"Dad, no!" Orion said. Finally, a reaction from the boy.

"No," Pedro shouted back. "You guys are fully capable. Goodnight."

He tapped Telegram open. Almost all of his BOWC friends had replied with video and voice messages on the community thread.

Hang in there, P! We love you, okay? You'll get through this.

Maybe take the family camping? I can set you up with a great spot.

Let's talk about going native. You can do it with your whole family.

Then, a private message from Tanya. She was divorced. Two kids herself. She and Pedro had been *talking*. They'd gone out for coffee once, but there wasn't a lot of spark. She had been close with Shelly, before she went native. Pedro felt that Tanya was treating him like a widow, which he wasn't. He was simply…abandoned.

Look, I know it's tough. My kids—I just had to pull the plug. We went cold turkey about a week ago. My thirteen-year-old literally tore the house apart looking for his phone and tablet. We're going to New Mexico for a while to stay on my sister's ranch. She's got thirty acres near Angel Fire. They need to detox. Maybe that's what you guys need. It's not going native, but it's a chance to reconnect. Think about it. Let me know. We're just waiting for the weather to clear up in that part of the country, then we're driving out. I'm taking a sabbatical from work. I'm going to homeschool them.

That crazy thing that always happens after extended breaks from school happened again on January 3. Axel and Orion suddenly fell ill with something. Aches, pains, nausea. When these symptoms appeared, Pedro ignored them. They'd grumble and moan, then Pedro would hold the tablets over them, threatening to take them away, which forced some compliance, at least it would get them in the car, but then they would lean into their psychosis and the physical symptoms would manifest. Orion had mastered puking on demand. Axel's skin went flush and clammy and he went catatonic. If Pedro played cool, he might get both of them to exit the car and go to school, but usually they alternated and he never knew which one would play it worse. He often wondered if they planned it out the night before, who would be the lucky one in the morning to stay home.

That morning, it was both and Pedro did not play it cool. In the parking lot, he lost it.

"Get the fuck out of this goddamned car or I swear to God I'll lose my fucking shit. I have to go to work. Now, get out!"

Orion had thrown up twice already, the stench rising from the passenger seat where he had aimed, Pedro trying to catch it in a Trader Joe's bag. Axel snapped out of his trance and rolled down his window, declaring "This is child abuse!" so other parents and students could hear. Pedro rolled up the windows and locked them, locked the doors, and then drove off. He pulled over to send a message to their teachers that the boys wouldn't be in today, to please send him their assignments.

His attempt to quickly cool himself down turned into a cold silence, which he had mastered with them. He had been an expert at it when Shelly was still around. It got him—them—nowhere. It was a symptom of a much larger problem in their family, one that Shelly resolved one night on her own when she set out, perhaps into Ruffin Canyon herself to eschew technology forever.

Going native wasn't only for members of the Benevolent Order of Woodland Creatures. Humans by the thousands were exiting their homes and workplaces and towns and cities and countries and leaving no trace behind. Bank accounts remained open and active and identification cards remained in purses and wallets wherever they had been left. But some people took theirs. Some people did the responsible things and closed up accounts and paid off debts and wired money where it needed to go. Like Shelly. She was smart. She wasn't going to shit in the woods. Some people turned up in other countries across the world and began living their new lives. Pedro's closest neighbor and former drinking buddy, Chris Le, had sent Pedro a random email about eight months after Chris had apparently gone native. Chris was living in Thailand now, working at a resort.

"Inside," Pedro told the boys.

They were in tears, their shirts soiled.

"Go take showers," he said.

"We'll do our homework, Dad," Axel said.

"You listen here," Pedro said. "Don't you ever say I'm abusing you. Do you hear me? Do you hear me? Now go get cleaned up."

Orion approached Pedro, reaching for his dad's hand. Pedro pulled away.

"I'm sorry," Orion said. "I just didn't feel well."

"Look," Pedro said. "I don't care what you do today. Play your games, do your work. Whatever. I'm done. I'm just done. I'm done with this. With you. With all of this. I'm so sick and tired. I just. I just need to go lie down, okay."

The boys cried and Pedro, though not happy to see what he had done to them, relished in the fact that they were, at last, showing real human emotions. He went up to his room, logged into his work computer, and set his profile to out of office. He shut his phone off and when the boys came to his locked bedroom door, he told them to come back later. He spent the rest of the day packing essentials. Clothes. Blankets. Toiletries. He would collect food and water that night before he set out. Alone.

The silence of the home signaled him to emerge from his room. It was 1:45 a.m. He never heard them put themselves to bed that night. He was going to peek into their room, but that would be too hard. Too much to do in the moment. He'd have to cut ties. Just the way Shelley had. *How could someone do that? Stop. Don't think of that. Of her. Of them. Save yourself.*

In the kitchen, under the dim light of the range top, he worked quickly gathering bars and snacks, filling his water bottles. He'd drive to the Anza-Borrego desert, camp for the night, then check out what was happening in Desert Hot Springs. Rifling through the food stuff and packing, he knew exactly how Shelley could do that. Her job as a parent was rendered useless. The machines were now raising the children. Not a mother, or a father. And even their attempts at governing the modems—setting strict hours of usage and downtime—didn't work. The boys figured out how to work around it. They found the passwords, they gained access, and lost what was left of their childhood. That's what drove her away, and perhaps the guilt for putting the screens in front of them in the first place. Holding that notion that kids grew out of things, that they would find other pathways. Their ideas of free range were so vastly different. Perhaps one day she'd turn up, like Chris in Thailand, living her best new life. Pedro believed he deserved one, too.

He turned on his phone, only to check the drive time then leave it behind, but he had several messages from Axel sent within the Warpath app. Pedro ignored them and turned the phone off. He grabbed his keys, and wedged into the keyring was a handwritten note.

Dad, can you help me with my injection in the morning? I know I can do it, but I need your help. Plz.

Pedro held the note, studied it, bit his lip. He hadn't cried like that in a long time. He turned on his phone again, tapped the Telegram app. Tanya was online.

Tanya, sorry to bother you so late, but if you're up, please tell me how to do it. How can I get out of here with them? They're going to have so many withdrawal symptoms. I'll go with you. We'll go with you. To New Mexico.

She soon replied with a video message. Smiling, laughing, dispatching from the darkness of her bedroom.

It's funny. I'm up. I've been in a little insomnia phase. It might be best to take them in the night. Like right now. Just wake them and say there's an emergency and you have to get out of the house in a hurry. Pack it all up and start the car and then rush them out of the house. They'll be so disoriented they won't even know what to do, or to think of their devices. Or if they ask for them, tell them you packed them already. Then start driving. I'll text the address. I'll tell my sister your coming. And hey, just call me. Okay? Bye.

Pedro doubled up on the food, grabbed their dirty clothes hampers in the garage. He'd wash later. He loaded the car with more blankets, pillows. Extra water. He packed Orion's doses, then kicked the tablets under the couch, not before smashing the screens with a hammer. He turned on the car in the driveway and sat in the driver's seat for a minute—alone—then he got out, ran upstairs, shouting, turning lights on.

"Wake up. Wake up, guys. We gotta go. We gotta go, boys."

THE BREAKFAST HOUSE

March 12, 2028

The girl doesn't cry anymore. The boy, however still does. It's all too fresh in his memory, and for a boy to lose his mother, at his age, is like scaring a kitten. It will forever be spooked, destined to jump at the slightest *boo!* We shouldn't refer to them as the boy or the girl, but that was what we did. It was a means to amuse ourselves. We had started bingeing the old shows. *I Love Lucy, Leave it Beaver.* When Ward and June weren't calling him Beaver, they called him the boy. As in, "don't be so hard on the boy." What was Wally? Wally was a boy, too. But they didn't call him that. Nor did they have a rodent nickname for him. He was just Wally. Maybe he was too close to being a man to call him *the boy.*

And so it just stuck. But our boy—Kip—he's still a boy, even though he's twelve now and starting to get more angular with the tiny once blonde whiskers around his upper lip and jawline starting to get a little darker by the day, a preview of what might be a beard someday. We even caught him flirting a while back—before all of this—at the tot pool. Jasmine, the singer, was there with her niece and she said to Kip, "You're very sweet with you little sister there. It's good to see you doing that."

Kip said back to her, "It's good to see you, too."

He's a charmer, that boy, Jasmine had said.

ANIMAL HUSBANDRY

We started watching the really old shows because we ran out of ideas. That and we had watched all the new ones in rapid succession, as though scrolling the phone, just watching and watching and watching. Plus, the next show just starts up again, so you kind of have to watch it. That was of course, when the power was on. When it was on, we kept the TV on, and when the TV was on, we watched.

Kip and Lise would stay up with us—we stopped bedtimes fairly early on during the Outage—and they had lots of questions.

"This is what life used to be like," we would tell them.

"Why did they only have black, white and gray clothes?" Lise asked.

She's a smart one. The fact that she included gray was adorable. It had been a legitimate concern of mine too when exposed to those shows as a kid, that was until my parents had told me about technicolor. It was amazing that we had advanced from something like *Leave to Beaver* to *Gilligan's Island* in just a few years.

I don't know, I guess me and Kelani were feeling nostalgic. Everyone is. Everyone wants to go back to something. I want to go back to when she was alive. It feels like she's going to just walk in any minute, like she's been on a vacation or a work trip. She travelled quite a bit with work. It's like those times when she would leave on a trip, and how there was a palpable emptiness left in her absence, as though her energy was still there, but now that feeling is fading.

When the Outage first happened, all of we neighbors had Friday afternoon happy hours in the courtyard driveways. It was like bar hopping. Someone suggested doing the meals that way. Someone took the dinners, others the lunches. We volunteered for breakfast. It worked out nicely because in those days, when Kelani came to my Trader Joe's, she seemed to buy only breakfast foods. Cereal, shelf stable milk, bacon—which we froze, eggs and prepared eggs in the carton, which we also froze, bread, butter, syrup, and shredded potatoes.

I began stocking up, too, always bringing home extra groceries after my shifts. I also began buying batteries. At one point, we had bought more batteries of all sizes than we knew what to do with, and then after a while, all of them were gone. I also read everything I could about the Outage. So much so that in the quiet hours late at night, after the kids were asleep and we had time to ourselves, Kelani would end conversations about the Outage, saying that one day all the power was just going to come back on the way it used to.

The food was one thing, and the fact that I was suddenly a single dad was another. That seemed to be why everyone wanted to visit. Early on, and after Kelani died, I had to clear things up. Be transparent. No, I had said to the neighbors, neither I nor Lise or Kip were there. We didn't see the accident. And that's all it was, an accident.

We are well and healthy, I told the neighbors, and we would love company. We can still be the breakfast house. Serving breakfast only was perfect for Lise. She's still such a picky eater. The girl will only eat breakfast. Kids can eat Cheerios all day every day. It's the perfect apocalypse food, provided you have milk, of course.

Not everybody has power. That's been the strangest part of all. Sometimes it's on, other times it's not. When it's on, it's on for a few days and things feel like nothing has happened. Other times it's off, and it's off for days. Weeks. And then it's as varied from house to house, street to street, town to town, state to state, country to country. There's no consistency. It's like one massive flickering out.

Kelani went for a walk during one of the longer blackouts. The one which forced us to use flashlights for a few weeks at night. When there was no internet, no TV, no phone, no nothing in our part of town. It was when the fog had rolled in from the coast. We rarely get it as far inland as we are.

In those early days, our place was one of the few that retained electricity with some regularity. I realize now that our neighbors coming over so often was just so they could eat, plug in, survive. Before all of it, we hardly knew them. We only exchanged meager hellos and waves as quickly as we could entering and exiting our garages and front doors as people do in California.

At one point they were coming over as early as 6 a.m. for coffee. I didn't fire up the griddle until 8 or so, but I told Ted next door to go ahead and let himself in to start the coffee. I even gave him our door code. Kelani didn't like that. She never trusted Ted. She said there was just something about him. One time, she tried to introduce him to her mother when she visited us from Portland, but it was like there was absolutely zero chemistry there—like two robots meeting. I haven't been able to get through to Linda. She knows about Kelani. She wrote back to an email I had sent. She wasn't able to get out of Portland because of the power. They haven't had power since just after the beginning, or so we've heard.

It's the lack of information everybody talked about at the breakfast table.

Why are we not told anything?

Is this just happening here?

No, Chicago is fine, Ted had said. So is Oklahoma City, Raleigh, upstate New York. Other cities. Ted works for the government—he never says exactly what—so we hung on his every word. Thing is, we didn't get much from him. He would take his coffee, go to work, then come back late. He used to bring back jugs of gas for folks on the circle, which was super helpful, and he promised to keep my tank full for all the coffee drinks, and because I'm alone with the kids.

March 29, 2028

So that's what it's been. A hobbled-together set of good days and bad days. It's like the rules are suspended, and on the one hand it feels good, but on the other hand it's awful. You don't know where you stand. Every night, Lise would ask me, "School night?" She stopped asking a while ago.

Kip keeps to his room but comes down for breakfast. He mingles a little bit if neighbors come by.

And so, I keep writing. I keep at this. Why, why, why?

Because I don't know how to do anything else.

Kip knows it, but he doesn't want to talk about it. I don't want to talk about it either. It's like we both know it and will probably go on knowing it for the rest of our lives and maybe we'll never talk about it. Maybe Lise will figure it out. But she's so young, she'll forget everything. She'll never remember that she was, at one time, a prop. If the power ever comes back on and stays on, maybe when she's a teenager or something, she'll remember what her mother used to do and she'll think—Instagram, I remember that. Mom used to do that.

I shouldn't call Lise a prop, but goddamn it, that's what she was. Kip was too, to a lesser extent. There was a period of time when they were both willing subjects for Kelani. They would smile and pose and work for the camera. They'd "do it for the 'Gram." But then Kip started to check out at about ten years old. The schtick wore off. And it was about that time that Kelani was in so deep, I hardly saw her without her phone. She lived life through that lens. The phone had basically become her hand. She spoke to it. Spoke into it. She went to bed with it and woke up to it. We would go places and people would stop her and say you're *MomDotCom*! We love your posts! I'm here because of you! You influenced me!

Our scheduled sex times (Sunday afternoons, between 4 and 6 pm) were the only times we really connected, but even then, it wasn't very…loving. It was like something she needed to check off her list. The scheduled sex was her idea. It was one she proposed early on. She never really liked the spontaneous stuff, plus, she had a no tickling/caressing rule, so that left a lot off the table. I honestly can't remember how we "found" each other sexually in the first place. I think it was after a few first dates when she said she wanted to have sex, and from then, it was mostly on her terms.

In recent years, there wasn't a single family outing that wasn't a production. I started counseling because I thought I was the one with communication issues, but I didn't realize she was the one with an addiction. A bona fide, honest-to-god, addiction. Maybe I didn't give her the attention she needed. Maybe it was why she turned to the phone and the fans. I thought for a long time that there was someone else. I even scoured her followers one night looking for creepy dads or other dudes. But there wasn't someone else. There was *something* else: what she had built, and like any monster, it had to be fed. Not daily, but by the minute.

And so when all this power, all this buzzing electricity around us—the thing that keeps us checking in and checking up and keeping score and posing and pretending and just wasting our time living for a screen stopped, she didn't know what to do. There was no way to plug in. There was no way to post. Or, if there was, it was inconsistent. It was here and there, not every night or every morning. The comments stopped. The outings ceased. There was nothing to share. Everyone was experiencing this other thing, this mysterious Outage.

And the drinking had always been there. I didn't think that was a bad thing. A few drinks after dinner to unwind. A few more at holidays. Then the bottles showed up. That was when I noticed an uptick. And at the events and parties and pre-shows and back stages and meet-the-cast and the photo ops with the characters, there was always a bar with a rosé or a signature cocktail or something and she never said no. In the run up to this Outage, it was like *The Great Gatsby*. It's like the world might have known that this was the last hurrah. Get your snap shots now, because it's all going to go away like that, bitches.

I don't mean to use the word bitch. She wasn't a bitch, that's not what I mean. But she wasn't Kelani. She was MomDotCom. She was a character herself. What she wanted to be. And what she eventually became. She lived in that world and all the thousands of followers who were holding her up made her what she was. And maybe she liked being that person. Maybe she liked herself. It was hard to say. We didn't talk deeply in those final weeks. Maybe even months, or now that I think about it, years. I was busy working and raising the kids and she was…looking for a good shot.

That's why she went for a walk that night. She'd finished off the last of the egg nog liqueur she'd bought for the holidays. The early February rains had come and gone, and come again, and in between were those foggy nights with no power, no internet, no one to connect with but your own family. And that was when she went for a walk.

And in a time of global upheaval, the news doesn't stop for the demigods of social media. They don't comment that a beautiful woman in the prime of her life known as MomDotCom to thousands of followers was struck down in the fog by a reckless driver with no lights on during one of the longest stretches of the blackout. They don't comment on that because there was no news to watch. No place to post.

I didn't know her passwords and my face wouldn't open her phone. I couldn't post anything to let the fans know. The phone still sits on the little charging station where she kept it on her nightstand, and it's almost like it's her. It's like her whole existence is in there and what's left is a timeline of all the fun she orchestrated over the past how ever many years, with that last abrupt stop on December 14, 2027, when we hugged Mickey and Minnie Mouse before Disney on Motherfucking Ice. The power went out on January 1, 2028.

April 8, 2028

Kip comes in every morning to wake me. He's become my little alarm clock. When Kelani was alive, she was my alarm clock. She woke me by always leaving our bedroom door wide open and starting breakfast at about 6:30 am. That was in the normal times. When the kids went to school. She was always the early riser. We joked that I would need one of those beds that shakes to get me out of it. But once I was up, I was up, and I fell in line with the family chores or to get ready for work. And then she was off to her job, just down the hall in the home office, where she held what was called a full-time job as a pharmaceutical rep, but it became more of a part-time job as the social media began actually pulling in resources. And me, someday going to sell that screenplay by late night, Lyft driver by morning, Trader Joe's stock boy by night. I'm lucky if I get a shift anymore. The screenplay: haven't even looked at it in months.

This morning, Kip tapped me and I tossed and turned for a while, and then eventually I woke up and when I looked over, he was pecking away at Kelani's phone. For the longest time I thought he was just playing with it, until this morning when I realized he was actually using it. He was scrolling it, pretty sure on her IG account. He tossed it aside when he noticed me watching him. I asked him if he knew the password and he denied it at first, but he gave it to me later. 041191. How the hell had I not figured it out? Kip's birth month, Lise's birth month, Kelani's birth year. I swear I had tried that, or a combination thereof, on the million times I tried to unlock her phone, but after all those attempts, it locked for several weeks, and so, I just forgot about it.

I feel like I'm talking to Mom when I use it, he says.

I know, buddy, I know.

And now, I know. I'm in. I'm in her phone. It's kind of like having access to an enormous filing cabinet: it's all in there somewhere, and it's messy, and you don't know where to start and it's also scary as hell. She kept meticulous files. Files and sub files. Multiple email accounts. Hundreds and hundreds of contacts. Thousands of texts. And more photos than there are grains of sand at the beach. I didn't do anything with it for a while because I didn't think I needed or wanted to. And then, the curiosity set in.

First, her Instagram. There were hundreds of messages of concern, worry, dread.

Is everything okay?

We haven't heard from you in forever???

This outage is crazy! Any news?

Oh my god, I think I heard you were hurt?

I just heard that you died? Is this true??? OMG!!!!!

We had a small service at a funeral home. Neither of us were religious, so we didn't have much of a faith community. Our neighbors came, as did my shift mates from TJ's. They knew because we were connected in the store on the days it was open. A lot them knew about Kelani's page, but in the end, none of the followers came, and it's sad, because she didn't really have many friends. Her hair stylist, esthetician, and some older ladies she used to work with at the mental health hospital showed up. At the tiny candlelit ceremony we had, I swear I overheard something awful. I think it was whisper from a neighbor or coworker. It was something like: I'd rather have a few really good friends than a thousand followers. In air quotes. Fucking air quotes.

April 14, 2028

I had to put it away. I couldn't respond to all of it. It was just too much. And would they even get the response? Most times, when I used the app, the message said it was trying to finish loading. The internet isn't what it used to be. I never really cared, because I didn't have a single account. I once created a Reddit to read an article a friend had texted me, but the whole thing gave me headache. I've always thought the hobbies and interests and whatever we do are actually preparing us for something. I suppose my lack of connection to the social media monster was good training for this unending technology drought. I do miss the Lyft dings, telling me there's a ride waiting. I used to go out for shifts, but after a while, it was pointless.

April 30, 2028

Kip wants to log into her phone every morning. After a while I said why the hell not. He started showing Lise, but she lost interest fast. It's like Kelani is being erased from her memory. We didn't put a lot of pictures up—neither of us were much for decorating—so there's nothing anchoring Lise to the family unit. Lise plays with some girls down the street, and I'm watching them turn a little feral. Kind of like how kids used to be. Outdoor play for hours, return home when the sun goes down, scabs and scratches, no baths for days, water sometimes.

Kip still stays nearby. He suggested we revive the Instagram account. He said that we could keep MomDotCom alive. I'll consider, I told him. We might have to. Money is getting tight, although, money's becoming somewhat useless. Point of sale terminals are so inconsistent, not to mention the processing systems that actually execute the transactions go out for days, sometimes weeks at a time. On a shift I actually had at Trader Joe's a few weeks ago, I helped at the registers since we no longer stock the frozen stuff. We now write down people's names, what they bought, total it up with calculators, and then, *if* they come back, we take their card or their cash, but the terminals and processors have to be working, and so it's basically an honor system. We devised a plan where if their account is clear, they can shop. If not, they have to keep coming back and pay when things work. If not, they're banned. And that's where security comes in. That's where all the work is these days. Swole dudes have never been busier. Not paid well, but definitely in high demand. They're everywhere the martial law isn't, and that's most places.

May 3, 2028

I find myself unlocking her phone long after the kids have gone to sleep. Each night, it's like peeling an onion. One night it's the DM's, another night it's the photos, the next night—the text messages. There were a few mysteries. Some user on Instagram called @Yonder59. They shared a lot of messages. I can see that it's a woman. No activity for the last several months. They talked about a lot of things. It started out as tips about what to do around town, then it turned into personal things. *Why isn't your husband in the pictures? Are you married or single? How long?*

How's it going? Not bad, but not good. More like brother and sister than husband and wife. It became a bit of a commiseration session. Then it faded off. There were a few other exchanges like that with other followers. It was like an ongoing therapy session. One, I saw was a man. It was a barrage of compliments, and Kelani's response were just on the border of flirty:

oh stop!
You're too funny!
You make me laugh!
LOL
Nice pic!
Wow! (three heart emoji)

There was no way to see what they had exchanged in terms of pictures. Those had already faded into the black hole of the internet. What hadn't faded into the black hole of the internet were her photos. I spent hours looking at the family pics. I laughed and cried. I wanted to physically go into them, to return to those exact moments in time and never come back. Then, I found the hidden ones. I bypassed the FaceID with her code, and what I found was... I don't know what to say. Beautiful, artistic, sexy, vulgar, far too personal. But I keep asking myself why. I suppose all the time with a camera meant that she was curious and a bit of an exhibitionist. Did she share them? Were they for other people? Just her? Is that what people send when they say, "send nudes"?

I couldn't go back. I didn't want to go back. It was like seeing those old print porno mags for the first time. It's exhilarating and shocking, but it's forbidden and harmful, and there was something wrong about it—the mother of my children exposed like that. I just couldn't...

June 17, 2028

    I should give this up. Change the code to something I'll forget, but I keep looking. And why not? It's getting dangerous out there. More places are going offline. The government food programs are becoming like little war zones. We now shelter in place from 8 pm to 8 am. Ted said I should get a gun. I've never wanted one, and when I said I wouldn't know where to start, he said he could set me up. He's been our only breakfast customer of late, but it's only for coffee, and he doesn't even need to anyway because it's not even coffee every day. It's mostly tea when I get the burners to work, and an old-fashioned pour over coffee once in a while. When I asked him what's next, he said anything and everything, to prepare for the worst and best. I asked him if it's really solar winds that caused all this, and he said that's just the half of it.

July 3, 2026

    I'm done looking at this. I can't do it anymore. This isn't her. But then again, it's who she always was. The person I never knew. In an app I thought was nothing, was actually everything. It was some simple note taking thing. A minor icon. A nothing app. She'd been adding to it for years. Long before the Outage. It was all of her thoughts and fears and worries and anxieties—and her depression. It made sense now. She was using the MomDotCom thing to make herself feel better. Her depression looked like that: fun and light and always up to something, always in the know, always one step ahead of the others. But she was fragile and dying inside. She even admitted it, that she was diagnosed with it, but she kept it from me. But why? Why wouldn't she just let me know, or get some help? Why did she want to slog it out like that all on her own? I didn't do anything because I couldn't do anything.

Maybe it was how she was raised. Her tiger parents. Only handle it once, they said. Never ask for help. All this time she was hurting. Every day a struggle to put on a face, then put that face out for the world—her little world—to see.

She didn't hate me. But I'm not sure she loved me. There were several entries about how she was alive just to support her deadbeat husband and kids. I think she loved the kids, but it's hard to say how much. She spent pages saying how she fantasized about just leaving us all one day. She wrote over and over how much she thought she was a terrible parent and should have never had kids. How she was a terrible wife and didn't think marriage was really worth anything after a while. How she herself wasn't worth much anyway either.

But what was worse was how close she came to ending it all. In one of her entries, she said how when she parked in the mall in the underground lot one time, she considered backing up far into the lane, then pushing the gas pedal down as hard and fast as she could so that she could smash herself into the concrete wall. She'd narrowed it down to a few ways. Jumping off the Coronado Bridge, driving into something, or an overdose.

And then I found what was probably her attempt at her last note. Her official goodbye. Something about not feeling happy about anything, about not having a purpose. About having lost something for herself long before she became a wife or mother. She apologized over and over. She didn't want anyone to see her in the condition she would be found in. She apologized to the kids. *I'm sorry, I'm sorry, I'm sorry.*

I'll never know if it was just an accident.

August 29, 2028

    We finally laid her to rest today. It was the funeral we should have had. Just the three of us in a beautiful place. Sunset Cliffs. She had said to spread her ashes there if anything ever happened to her—that's about as close as we ever got to estate planning. But we never let go of any ashes because the crematoriums were out of service. The best they could do was a mausoleum. Her body's laid to rest at Cypress View, but that's not really her.

    Today, we recorded a video. MomDotCom's official sign off. I posted it but there wasn't a signal, so who knows if it went up. The kids will never now. They didn't seem to care either. Kip cried as usual. Lise frowned, then took more interest in the dirt when I started digging. I made the hole deep. At least four feet. We turned off the phone, kissed it, said goodbye, then buried it. I'll tell the kids someday that their mom was a troubled lady. Or not. It might not even matter.

    Back at our community, we decided to go to the pool at the clubhouse. That's one thing the association has kept up with even during this upheaval. It's never heated, but the surface is clean, and they've made sure to run the pumps for as long as they can when the power comes back on. It's starting to look a bit like a pond with a slight film of algae growing on the sides and bottom. But why not get in? We're saying that a lot these days.

    Lise stripped all the way down. I told her to at least put her bottoms on, but she shrugged and jumped in. She said she was a merperson, and I told her I liked that. I jumped in next, motioning to Kip. He wouldn't get in, only shook his head, and sat on the deck. We stayed until dark, the water actually got even colder despite it being a hot day. At about the time they used to turn on, around 8 p.m., something happened. The underwater lights flickered on and stayed on. Then the light posts that lined the perimeter of the pool deck, the brown painted cylinders with little vents on the top, came to life, too. The lights of the gym went on, and just then Kip stood up. He stared ahead, eyes blinking, trying to focus on something over the cinderblock fence.

Dad, he said, I see lights from the shopping center across the street. They're on! He said. They're on!

MEDICINE BOX

Around the steady burning fire, Pascal Blas Leon stood, the flames illuminating his gaunt, bearded face. It was late October and the air was cold near the old John Dunn bridge of this part of the Rio Grande, just north of Taos, New Mexico. The other faces around the fire included his wife Tina, and their son and daughter Victor and Juana, the twins, now sixteen years old, along with twelve other *viajeros*. Travelers. They were from all over the Southwest, most from New Mexico, some from Arizona, California, the former Texas Republic, and Colorado. All were Native American or Latino people—the Dusty People—they were once called as a group in those unforgiving times. They waited, watched Pascal. He had just described his lineage to them. Twelve generations of Norteños—those from Santa Fe north—a mix of San Ildefonso Pueblo, Spanish, Mexican, and a sprinkling of other European. He knew of some Basque and German somewhere really far back.

"I'm brown and proud. I may not look it sometimes. Hell, sometimes people think I'm Middle Eastern, sometimes Greek, but that's me. That's us. We're the world's longest line of mutts."

The travelers laughed.

"We come here tonight to talk about two distinct moments in time: the past, and the future. We also come here to talk about two states of the future. Dystopia and utopia. I won't go too far into the past. That's up for you to research. Spend time knowing where you come from. Spend time learning the stories of your family, your ancestors. You are standing on their shoulders right now. Know them by name and call to them, whomever they are, good or bad.

"I want to thank my father, Blas Pascal Leon Sr., for helping show me the way. For helping show me the medicine of our ancestors right here in New Mexico, and for sharing the ways of the ancestors of our distant brothers and sisters in South America. We're all connected, and my father helped me understand that. In my family, he researched our relatives and found that we had a common ancestor, that my great-grandfather, whose name was also Blas, was an apprentice curandero who learned from an elder in Mexico. That elder, and my great-grandfather worked with the *hongo*—the mushroom. You see, we're all telling the same story over and again, and history is repeating itself over and over. It's our jobs to pay attention to how it's repeated and to shape it so that the bad stuff doesn't happen again.

"So. What about the bad stuff. I'll start by saying that long, long ago, people—all people—no matter your skin color or gender or sex or anything, had full control of their bodies. They had the right to honor and defend their bodies any way they wanted. Over time, that changed. Different cultures within different lands and countries made rules and regulations, or put in place religious dogmas that forced one segment or another of any given population to do certain things to their bodies or prevent their bodies from doing certain things. You've heard of male and female genital circumcisions, castration, chastity belts, abstinence, forced pregnancies, restrictions on terminating a pregnancy, forced vasectomy, castration once again. It all seems to come full circle.

"Around the time that my father, Blas Pascal Leon Sr., was apprehended by US Customs, then forced into his vasectomy, I knew I was going to be in trouble. That I would be next. I was already practicing healing with him. I had returned from Peru after an ayahuasca retreat and my father was due to return home after me. But he wasn't so fortunate. They had our numbers. After he passed away, the Male Wellness Act administrators called me to say that I had been reclassified as a Zeta due to my association with my father and the practices I was engaging in. The practices of keeping the medicine alive. The practice of what we have just taken part of these last few days together.

"I had to act fast. Tina here, my fiancé at the time, and I looked for anyone who could help her get out of the country fast. Because I had just returned from South America, there was no way that I could leave again. They were going to find me no matter what. After quick research amongst other healers and lots of dark web scouring, we found a clinic that would take my semen, freeze it, then send it along with Tina. We booked her travel to London. In those days, it was quite easy to go from the US to the UK. Not a lot of questions asked. Tina flew to London with my sample and found a place to stay—to live—using the network of healers there. London, most of Europe, was much more hospitable to people in our plight. She lived there for the next five years, while I stayed here. I stayed here, went through the procedure, but I fought. I kept fighting. I was doing what my father said to do: use non-violence. Use my head. Be strong. Stay principled.

"Meanwhile, Tina became pregnant and eventually gave birth to our twins here. I met them in person when they were just about to turn five years old. That was the time our government had shifted back to the old ways, the more balanced and more humane ways. Not the old true ways. The ancient ways. That's what we're rebuilding here, one day at a time. But we know it will never be the same. We'll all have those memories. Those scars. We'll have to work much longer, apply more medicine, more salve, to help ease that pain. Every day, when I see my children, when I'm able to be with my family, I ease that pain. I think of how what was once dystopia, is now coming back into balance. Is it utopia? I don't think so. It may never be. Our world—our universe—demands black and white, hot and cold, yin and yang. There will always be opposing forces of good and evil. Our job is to recognize both and understand where their place is, and where we fit in between. Our job is to remain vigilant and hopeful. It's a delicate balance.

"Now, before our *risa terapia*, before we close this weekend with laughter and tears, I want to thank you for giving me this space to share my story. Thank you for listening. And now, I'd like to invite you to turn to those around you, and tell them something, or simply show them that you care, that you love them with all of your heart. If it's all taken away again, all we have is our hearts."

*

"My father was in Peru at the time. When he was on his retreats, he didn't check his phone or email or anything. He came back to reality on his terms, you know? I mean, plus, he'd been there for months. He was deep in the medicine."

Pascal laughs, but it's an uncomfortable chuckle. He's too young to have his father's crow's feet, so when his smile drops, the skin around his eyes pulls taught around his orbitals. He seems, however, to have aged just a bit more on this interview.

"So, what was the first thing he learned about the new Male Wellness policy? How did he find out?" Alistair Coombs, the host of *Set in Stone* said.

"He had landed in Los Angeles before his connecting flight to Albuquerque when he called me to tell me they had arrived early. He said he was about to go through customs. I said, 'Pa, I don't think you should just yet,' and he laughed it off. He was obviously still in his bliss trance. He was always like that after the ceremonies. I said, 'Dad, no. There's been some—changes in this country. Big changes.'

"I tried to explain the Male Wellness Act. I tried to jog his memory that just before he left, the bill was going through the House. That those wackos were going to soon start classifying men into groups. He just laughed again. *'No te preocupes,'* he told me. I said, 'Dad, this is serious. Now, we're all either alphas, betas, sigmas, gammas…it's for real now' I told him.

"I sent him an article, but I could tell he was already going through. I had heard a voice telling to put his phone away."

"And that was the last you had heard from him?" Alistair said.

Pascal looked out into the invisible audience.

"Yeah. Before the change."

"And so, thinking of that moment, what were you experiencing? What were you personally going through, with all the changes?" Alistair said.

"I was still in shock. I was still processing it all. I was happy, I guess, that I wouldn't have to have The Procedure, but I was still entirely disgusted by it. That we had arrived here. That we had been sorted into some twisted fraternity system."

Alistair turned to the invisible audience, and as an aside, explained.

"The Procedure was forced vasectomy for those males deemed non-Alpha, Delta, or Sigma. And for those in need of a refresh of the Male Wellness Act Ranking System, the castes were as follows:

A large screen behind Alistair and Pascal illuminated, displaying seven tiles with seven images and word headings. The words were the Greek letters spelled out: Alpha, Beta, Sigma,

Gamma, Omega, Delta, Zeta. Seven distinct depictions of men appeared under the letters. Under the Alpha, was a large, physically fit man in business clothes with a serious, borderline angry expression framed by a trim beard and angular features. Under Beta, was a man of average build, wavy hair that hung at his ears wearing glasses over a serene face, his chest covered by a cardigan sweater. For Sigma, a man in outdoor gear appeared. His build was fit and strong looking, yet his face signaled inquisitiveness and skepticism. Delta showed a younger man in exercise clothing, flexing his muscles, his face bright with wonder and awe. Under Gamma, an everyday man appeared dressed in dark, baggy clothing, his face expressionless, almost lost. Under Omega was a thinner man, slopped shoulders, wearing long hair and colorful tattoos on his arms, his smirking face covered by a patchy beard. And lastly, Zeta, under which appeared the youngest man of all, looking far off into the distance, his thick curly hair stacked on his head in a type of stylized mullet, framing his almost feminine bone structure. As a whole, this gallery of men's faces resembled a wall of taxidermy, animal heads forever severed from their bodies, preserved for the world to stare at.

"After the Male Wellness Census, I received a notice that I would need to be interviewed. A lot of my friends and family at that time simply received their rankings after the census, but not me. I kind of had a feeling they were going to ask for more. The interviewer met me at my job. I was working at a plant nursery at the time. My title was Yard Help. Anyway, that's not the point. The point was this man, very Alpha looking, comes to my job and we go sit down near the fountains where there were some benches. His name was Tim Parker. Straight out of MAGA central casting. Remember those folks? The MAGA people? Anyway, he opened his tablet and began asking several questions."

"Care to share?" Alistair said.

"Things like where I was from, where my parents were from. How I grew up. Family traditions. Then he started asking about my interests and lifestyle, future aspirations, then onto sexual tastes and preferences. He kept saying, 'answer as truthfully as possible,' but yet—and I forgot to mention this—before he started the interview, he put a monitor on my forefinger. He straight up told me it was a lie detector, so I guess I didn't really have a choice, you know?"

"So, how did you fare? On the questionnaire?"

"Fine. I told the truth. I told him my father was Latino of Mexican and Peruvian descent, my mother first-generation Jamaican. I told him I'd only been attracted to women, that I had had a few girlfriends, nothing really serious. I told him I wanted to study botany. I told him I traveled a lot with my family, my father, and that I was my father's apprentice. That was when it got weird," Pascal said.

"Invasive. He wanted to know where and when I had gone with my father, and what my father did. That's when I told him my father was a shaman. It felt like the interview stopped then and there."

"Then what?" Alistair asked.

"He gave me my ranking. Delta-Gamma. But, he said I was low on Delta and high on Gamma, but that the two of them sort of balanced each other out. That Delta wasn't dominant enough for me to be full Delta. He said I wouldn't have to get The Procedure, but that they would follow up in three years or sooner. That it could change over time. Like, what the fuck, you know?

"But, then he said he wanted to follow up with my father directly, and that's when I told him he was out the country. I messed up on that one, because the next few weeks, they kept calling and emailing me, but I just ignored him."

"Absolutely stunning," Alistair said. "What else? Did you know other men impacted by these changes?"

"Oh yeah, sure. Lots. One of my closest friends was given Zeta, and he was quote—*scheduled*—for The Procedure within days of his notice. And by scheduled, I mean he got it without even knowing. He said all he remembered was going to sleep one night and then he woke up a day or so later in a jockstrap and with an icepack on his scrotum. In his own bed! He believes he was drugged at his employer that afternoon, or it might have been something he ate, like a sedative in his meal. He believes they did the procedure in his home. It was all so intrusive. I heard that they did that with Zetas. I had another friend who was ranked as a Beta, nice guy, but he was a registered sex offender. A long time ago, he had relieved himself at the beach when he was drunk and a family saw it and reported him and he was arrested then later went on the sex offender registry. After the Census, he was apprehended from his home, got The Procedure, and then—I'm sure you heard about these things—he was put in a Limping Belt."

"Those were the, ah—" Alistair pantomimed a brace over his own genitals.

"Yes, those. They kept men from even touching themselves." Pascal looked down and shook his head.

"It's just...shocking that it came to that. In the United States," Alistair said, also shaking his head. "And what about the men that were spared. I'm sure you knew some. What were they going through?"

"It's funny...actually, no. It's not funny. It never was. And why do people always say, *it's funny* just when they're about to say something that isn't funny?" Pascal lifted his head up, looked out into the nothingness of the empty recording studio. "Yeah, I knew a lot of guys—a lot of men—that weren't put through that nonsense. And they were the typical guys that fit those profiles: strong, big, jobs in the trades, doctors, surgeons, airline pilots. I knew them but I didn't *know them* know them. I didn't know them personally, is what I'm saying, but I knew of them, because they became the new face of the country. They were put on pedestals and practically worshipped. And it was pretty damn coincidental that they were, well, let's just say monochromatic."

Alistair threw his head back and laughed. "The U.S. never said it was a racist country, but I suppose they never said they weren't a racist country."

"Exactly," Pascal agreed. "I knew that had something to do with my father being apprehended."

"So, talk more about that," Alistair said. "Your father returns to the U.S., he goes through customs, then what?"

"Well, he was interrogated, strip searched, humiliated, then hauled off to a detention center. It took me days to figure all of this out, to even know where he went. It was a nightmare. There were no straight answers. It was 'call this department,' 'call that department,' 'fill out this form, that form.' Finally, I got through to an agent who I guess had some pity and told me people coming from overseas were being held in a detention center at the border. Why there, I have no idea. She told me it could take several weeks before they conducted the census then decided what to do with the men. She said they were processing arrivals as quickly as they could. She took my information and said she would relay a message and that they would send me updates. I think she took pity because I told her that it was my dad and that I had not talked to him in a while.

"Then, I finally received a message from him via email. I don't have the exact words, but it said something like, 'They got me. Damn near tortured me. Stripped me down, took all my books and papers and medicine. I guess I'm a Zeta, whatever that means. I'm supposed to go to some surgery center next week. What is going on here? If anything happens to me, please find my medicine box at home. It has everything in it you'll need."

"Before the medicine box, can you share what happened next to your father? Are you willing to share?"

"He was taken to that surgery center, and they, well, they gave him a vasectomy. A forced vasectomy. But he—he died. He died there."

"From the surgery?" Alistair said.

"Yeah, I guess. It was never explained fully. I'd like to think it was because he was older maybe, but he was a healthy fifty-seven-year-old. He was fit and strong."

"Which begs the question, why would they give him a vasectomy in the first place?" Alistair said.

"Right. Men who were either past they sexual prime or not even in relationships, or just gay still had to have one. It was the mandate. Those men were the threats to society."

"But not in the ways we might think," Alistair said.

"Yes, the Betas, Omegas, Gammas, and Zetas were ones who challenged society. They didn't fit into the mold they were creating."

"You say they. I suppose we should spend some time talking about *them*," Alistair said.

"Yeah. Them," Pascal said. "Why don't you start? You know enough about what happened as anybody else."

Alistair turned to the invisible audience. He was both host and dramatist in these moments. Commentator and curator of the past. That was what *Set in Stone* was about—examining where humanity had gone off the rails, where man had failed, but often course corrected.

"Thank you, Pascal. Yes. Let's talk about *them*. Friends, as we've discussed thus far, Pascal here is a descendant of one of the victims of the United States Male Wellness Act, legislated in 2047 by the AMG party. The AMG party itself a descendant of what was once the Republican party, which splintered in 2027 into the MAGA party and the GAP, or Great American Party. The AMG Party, or America Made Great party, came into power before the 2032 elections, just a few years after the Great Power Outage in the United States.

A visual of a timeline appeared on the large screen where the male stratification graphic once beamed. Alistair stood, pointing to the image like a weatherman, or the electoral college commentators of yore.

"Here we see the methodical rise of what was a minoritarian government taking hold at all levels of the political system, right down to the school boards in local communities. Over the course of a mere fifteen years, the work of both the MAGA and GAP parties gradually solidified what were considered red states into Christian Nationalist states that eventually overtook the electoral footprint. There was no turning back after that.

Alistair paused, then turned to walk a couple of paces on the stage. The timeline and map of red states behind him faded. His already somber face appeared more gray, more dramatic than before. The light over Pascal grew dim.

"On *Set In Stone*, we discuss heavy topics." Alistair stopped, looked forward with resolution. "We have conversations that are provocative and often disturbing. We have these conversations in order to elicit reaction, so that we do not repeat the same mistakes, so that we might find a better pathway forward. What happened in the United States for the better part of the 30's and 40's is indeed one that continues to be examined, and it is through

Pascal's account, as with many others that we have had on this show, that we're able to delve into this difficult period of time.

"What is so intriguing about this period of history is that it was almost straight out of a storybook. This period of time was, in fact, a near perfect example of life imitating art. In 1985, author Margaret Atwood published *The Handmaid's Tale*, a dystopian novel set in the future where an autocratic theocracy has taken over the United States and thus eliminated women's rights over their own bodies. Women in this society are the property of men and they live essentially cloistered for the purpose of reproduction. They are more or less reduced to sexual slaves in a patriarchal society.

"It could never happen here, right? Or anywhere, for that matter. At least that was the sentiment when the book was published, however the novel rose to popularity once again in the 20-teens triggered by the first Trump administration. A television series developed around that time, which stirred the population's imagination insofar that, again, a dystopian future as depicted in *The Handmaid's Tale* would not, and could not happen. That an energized society which systematically honored women's lives and women's bodies would not permit such a thing to happen. And yet. And yet.

Alistair moved dramatically to another mark on the stage.

"Imagine you were in a vehicle that was being built by that aforementioned minoritarian government and its base of supporters, that crucial third of the country. It's certainly not a popular vehicle, nor is it very functional, but it is moving forward no matter what. As it moves along, it gains more parts and thus begins to move faster, maybe not efficiently, but again, it moves forward with determination. It moves, picks up parts, gains attention—not popularity—but enough eyes begin to follow it. Reticular activators are activated, and over time, minds begin to change, and in turn, so do hearts. This is what makes change, good or bad. This is what happened in the United States with women's autonomy over their bodies.

Alistair now paced the stage.

"Now, suppose you remained in that vehicle over many years. One of the stops along the way was indeed a living version of *The Handmaid's Tale*. Perhaps not depicted exactly as it was in the novel, but the changes started small. Banned books. Prayers in school. The right to abortion stripped at a national level. While some people fled the country, others stayed. They began to bend, sometimes willingly, others against their will. It was those who didn't bend that received the most punishing blows. The line between church and state was virtually erased in hundreds of counties across the United States. That's where it started: in small blocks where the groupthink took hold, then eventually bolstered the political landscape.

"The origin point was perhaps Crook County in the state of Wyoming, where the head of the match ignited. Gerald Chesterton, a young boy, who, at the age of fifteen, began feeling out of tune with his body, shared with a close friend at school that he thought he might want to be a girl someday. That friend notified the school nurse in confidence, who then notified the principal. Gerald had never told his parents due to their deep religious convictions and political leanings, however they found out very soon when the school principal called them in for a meeting. What ensued was a firestorm starting with the school board unanimously deciding to separate boys and girls by grade. Separate boys' and girls' public schools came next. Soon after, the district revived, revised and eventually deployed a once outdated health and sexual education curriculum on that basis that only two genders exist, that heterosexual orientation is the only normal orientation, and that heteronormative gender stereotypes and roles must be upheld at all times. Layered on top of all of this was the gradual addition of prayer in school, as well as biblical teachings integrated into curricula in counties such as Crook in Wyoming.

"School districts in other traditionally conservative and far right states began to take notice and over time, began to implement their version of this structure. And this is how the movement took hold. Inculcate the children, and thus you create future generations of radicalized adults. While it would seem that traditionally liberal or left-wing states would resist and enact legislation against this kind of systemic change, the political environment was not in their favor. GAP party ideals, candidates, and eventually elected officials had pervaded city councils, councils of governments, state legislatures, secretaries of state, and state supreme courts, even in those states considered blue as per the old red, blue, and purple color coding used in those times. What replaced those once blue cities amongst red states, were patch works of crimson, the new color adopted by the GAP party.

"Next came GAP reform beyond primary schools. High schools, community colleges, universities in their previous forms, began adopting sex segregated and Christian educational norms, further solidifying the youth as followers of the growing Christian Nationalist movement. While liberal states like California, Massachusetts, and Illinois attempted to legislate bans on GAP ideals and principals, the situation became death by a thousand cuts. As more GAP officials took office in blue states, there was simply not enough political power to make meaningful and lasting change, plus, with an already weakened voter base that was too fragmented geographically beyond the major cities of the United States, balance in government was not in the foreseeable future. Add to this a plummeting population as hundreds of thousands of people with liberal and progressive leanings expatriated to Latin America, Canada, Europe and Australia. And it goes without saying that Unitary Executive Power had been in effect at the Executive branch of the U.S. government as ruled by the Supreme Court in 2037 during the Chandler administration.

"And so, we remain in that vehicle that was once impossible, once implausible, but one that became a sports car of sorts, zipping far and fast into the future, and at last, arriving at an analog version of Atwood's dystopia. Women's healthcare inverted such that childbearing was the only objective, and not the woman's overall health. Health systems built around preserving the uterus as a tool only for producing children, and "Nulliparous Penalties" for those who chose not to have children. Then eventually, that car arrived at the stratification of men, and the subsequent legislation of men's bodies."

The light above Pascal slowly rose, shining on his long, braided hair, his fedora, his woven poncho. The attire that had once been the cause of his own downfall.

*

"Remember when Dad used to give us his cast iron skillet fortunes?" Pascal lifted the lid off a dusty, compressed carboard cooler box. His father, Blas Pascal Leon believed in reusing everything. The cooler box once held the family's lunches on their many pilgrimages to the Chimayo Santuario every Good Friday. Years later, after Blas lost faith in the Catholic Church and started practicing curanderismo, he repurposed the box to store the medicine.

"Oh yeah," Natalia, Pascal's sister laughed. "It was all what he cooked that day. The greasier the meal, the shinier the pan."

"And the better the fortune," Pascal said.

"He was just making everything up as he went along," Natalia said.

Inside was a stratum of artifacts. Small plastic bags filled with herbs and resins, small colorful textiles, candles, matchbooks, Gua Sha stones, crystals, small tins with psilocybin tea bags, rolling papers, pipes both glass and animal antler, religious amulets like a pendant of the Virgin of Guadalupe plus several rosaries, a flask still full of mezcal, dried sprigs of hierba de romero and manzanilla, a journal, and several flash drives. The brother and sister had set out all the items on the dining table, its layout a miniature anthropology museum.

"These." Pascal reached for the flash drives. "This is where to start."

"Shit, where can we find a USB port?" Natalia said.

"I think I have one in an old technology box somewhere," Pascal said.

"Always holding onto stuff, just like Dad," Natalia said.

"Pretty much," he said. "Come on."

They went into the garage where Pascal had a wall of boxes, all labeled. Many his own medicine boxes that he pulled from often when he worked with people. He pulled the one labeled "Antique Cords & Shit."

"Do you think it's going to be okay?" she said. "To share all this?"

"I think it's what he'd want," Pascal said. "It's what he told me anyway. To open it. After he died."

"But if you go on that show. Do you think they'll...exploit it?" Natalia asked.

"No. I don't think so. His story needs to be told."

"I don't know. I just worry about some of those old GAP heads coming after us. After you?" Natalia said.

"Let 'em." Pascal opened the box and rifled through it, his hands surfacing with palmfuls of cords and cables, battery packs and adapters, dongles of all shapes and sizes, all of them nearly obsolete. "I'm not worried about them. They're ancient history. Well, not ancient, but you know, that time is over. We've evolved."

"Yeah, but they got you," she said. "Aren't you just a little bit angry?"

"Of course I am," he said. "But I don't waste my energy on them."

He fished out a white dongle whose female end would receive the USB sticks of the turn of the century. "Here."

They opened all of them, finding mostly PDFs of articles, scans of handwritten notes, typed documents, hundreds of pictures, and dozens of video clips.

"When did he have time to load all these?" Natalia said.

"He always found time. That's one thing that was truly magical about him."

Pascal clicked on a video file. On his monitor, an interview on Third Wave played. In the frame, Blas Pascal Leon Sr. and the host were on screen, their faces side by side in what was a virtual setting of the day. Pascal advanced the video a bit to show his father talking.

"I started practicing curanderismo to get back in touch with my roots," Blas Pascal Leon Sr. said. "My grandfather was a healer. He'd practiced in Mexico when he was younger, and though I was raised Catholic, I always had this calling to follow what nature is teaching us, not what a church says."

"You're known in the holistic medicine world as an ayahuasca shaman and sacerdote del Sagrado Masculino y Sagrada Femenina. Can you talk about those?"

"How much can I say?" Blas Sr. laughed with discomfort.

"As you know, we're all underground here. The passwords and triple factor authentications keep us protected, for now at least. Your wisdom is very much needed."

"Well, I'll share that the medicine has always been there, and it won't go away. At least outside of this country. And when the medicine calls you, you start to listen to it. You ask it questions. You contemplate it long before you actually commune with it."

"Always talking in codes," Natalia laughed, watching her father on the screen.

"Madre Ayahuasca called me very clearly one day when I was working in my yard in Arroyo Hondo in Northern New Mexico. It was like a voice…no, more like, a whisper. I had never been to Peru. Only read about it and saw it online, you know. But I received this clear vision of a valley, a green valley and a hut and this cloudy sky above it. I kept receiving this image whenever I was outside, and then one day I just decided to look up Peru. I went to the dark web, because, you know, they watch everything, and typed in Peru and there was that image. I found almost that exact image and it was tied to a shaman, who I eventually met and visited. I won't say their name, but that's what called me.

"And about el Sagrado Masculino y la Sagrada Femenina, I have to say that I have been a practitioner of it all my life, but I never knew it. I remember from a young age just feeling like I was not a man or a woman or anything, but more like a sexual being, if that makes sense. I did all the things you're supposed to do as a man, dated women, married, had children, and all the while I had this deep respect and understanding for both men and women, and some kind of connection to both, you know, like I knew what it felt like to be both. In the Native American world, that's called the Dual Spirit. I realized that's what I was and I was fine with it. My wife accepted it—eventually—and well, I became a leader in it, I guess. I started to help men with their identity crises and women with theirs. I helped women see that they were blessed with the vessel of the universe, that their wombs were doorways to the very spirit of the universe and that they were truly goddesses. I helped men understand that they were the givers of life and descendants of the creator itself and that they had to protect and serve all. I don't know, it's a lot to explain."

"No, I totally understand, and I applaud you for it," the host said. "You're keeping those traditions alive."

"Underground, but yes."

"Yes."

A palpable silence fell between them.

In real time, Pascal and Natalia looked at each other.

"Do you ever think you'll—get caught?" the host said. "For what you do?"

"I'm not scared of anything. If I'm caught, I'm caught. If it's my time, it's my time."

"Stop it there," Natalia said.

"I know. It's a lot," Pascal said.

"It was like he knew, but didn't know," Natalia said.

"What? That he was going to get caught?"

"Yeah, he was always saying that: 'if it's my time, it's my time,'" she said.

"That's how he lived life. He knew it was all going to end sometime." Pascal clicked on another file. It appeared to be an advertisement.

A carousel of images flashed, featuring Blas Pascal Leon and his offerings with their details. Eight day retreat in Peru. Dance ceremony in Mexico City. Plant and fungus workshop. Women's health services. All of it in coded language.

"Women's health services," Natalia muttered.

"Yeah, that's what did him in," Pascal said. He clicked on the next file. It was a news clip from the FCN network, a far right propaganda machine of the day. The brunette commentator started in with: "A so-called shaman out of the New Mexico territory is facing criminal charges for offering what one of his clients called an 'herbal abortion,' which left her hospitalized for weeks. Blas Leon is wanted for attempted abortion, and his so-called client, a Ms. Olga Macias is in custody with the Bernalillo County sheriff. We go now to our correspondent in the territory, Clive Howard, who is with the sheriff's department. Clive?"

Pascal closed the file.

"It's hard to believe we went back to being a territory, huh?" he said.

"I can't watch that," Natalia said. "I can't watch any of it."

"Yeah. I don't know what I'm going to say on the show," he said.

"Do what Dad would have wanted," Natalia said. "Open space, share your story, help yourself heal while you heal others. Everyone needs healing. We're all still healing from that time."

*

Pascal's Latin American travel authorization had arrived a week before his flight. He'd told his father maybe he wasn't going to make it after all, all the hoops he had to go through. Blas Leon, Pascal's father had said, "Our Jemez Pueblo cousins dance with hoops. Dance with your problems. Don't fight them. Just be patient. You'll get here when you get here."

Blas was now spending months at a time in Peru. He never said exactly where, one, to protect himself and the village he was in, and two, that's how Blas operated. One never knew fully what he was up to or where he was. Pascal's mother, Gloria, had spent many years, before she passed away, letting go of her husband piece by piece while standing by him. She had always joked that Blas had been going through a midlife crisis since he was in his twenties.

Getting out of the United States, especially to go to Latin America, required time, patience, and money. First, a petition to your congressional representative. Then applications to US Customs and Border Enforcement for the Travel Auths, visas, and bank statements. Then, a phone screening and possibly an interview with an agent. Then, deposits to Uncle Sam and usually the destination country. Peru only required $500 US for entry. The US required $1000 for exit. Pascal had used the story that he was visiting Peru for family ancestor research, and an immersive South American history course. He had provided the phone number and website to one of those decoy travel planners that could vouch for international travel if and when the US authorities audited the nature of trip, which was just about every time.

On the flight from Houston to Cusco, his longest in several years, his body rejected sleep, but when it came, he had a recurring dream sequence of being in London—a place he'd never been—having ceremony in a park. He was being blessed by a faceless medicine man, smoke pouring over him as the sun went down. Pascal shook off the dream every time, and he could already hear his father telling him that it was either the ancestors calling, or the medicine calling. Or, it was probably both. Damn it, it was both. Pascal was sure of it.

He was also sure that all those signs he'd been ignoring were definitely winks from the universe guiding him to the pathway of his father. It was like with any family business: the kids want nothing to do with it—at first. Or they do it but hate themselves for it. But, once they come around to it, they realize it's not so bad and hey, it's in my blood. Doctors produce more doctors, lawyers more lawyers, plumbers more plumbers, witch doctors more witch doctors. Rather, curanderos produce more curanderos. They only used that once in a while and as a joke only. Blas had told his son and daughter that he was not a witch and that they shouldn't use that word to describe what he did. Not that it was a bad word or that witches were bad. Witches certainly had their place, but he was not one of them.

On the ride to the village, Pascal's stomach began to turn. He hadn't eaten much, and still he felt nauseous. His Spanish was rusty, and he shocked the driver of the truck when he said to him that he, the driver, was making him disgusted, and not the drive itself that was making him sick. Pascal never forgot the word *asco*. Growing up, when the Osco Drug opened near their house, they joked that the drugs there were what made you sick. Nos dan asco. They make us sick. Later, Pascal would make the connection to what his dad was really trying to say: that pharmacy drugs disgusted him and that nature was the better way.

The sun was almost below the horizon when they arrived. Blas Pascal Leon Sr. was already standing there, outside of a small, thatched roof structure, ready to receive his son. The near twilight shone on the lush green ground cover and trees in every direction, creating an ethereal shimmer that was topped by a barely warm dewy humidity that wrapped around you like gauze.

"Welcome home, hijo" Blas said, pulling his son into his arms.

Pascal hadn't seen his dad in at least half a year. He hugged him back and took in the beauty around him. He was here, he was finally here.

"You look great, Dad," Pascal said, taking his father's sinewy frame in his arms.

"You look ill," Blas said. "It's the altitude."

Blas, always diagnosing, and always being right.

"I have tea," he said, "Come."

That night, after a light dinner of a black bean soup and more tea, father and son sat side by side contemplating the valley before them. Crickets making music with their legs, frogs in a haphazard chorus, and other deep throated birds with their hoots and calls filled the night sky. Pascal missed this, the unwatched feeling of being outside of the United States. He debated when to share the news with his dad, and which news should he share first.

"It's quiet tonight," Blas said, "but tomorrow will be very different. Tomorrow they arrive by the truckload."

Blas lifted his chin over toward the small structures where Pascal had arrived.

"Americans, mostly. Right?" Pascal said.

"Yeah, some Europeans. Australians. All gringos." Blas smiled. "That's why I'm glad you're here."

"Because you need more color?" Pascal laughed.

"Because you need to know about this, from the ancestral side. All these Americans, Europeans—let's just say Caucasians—they're broken. They need healing. Their ancestors only gave them more hard work and belief in Jesus, and look where it's brought them," Blas said.

"Yeah. You don't want to know what's going on in the US right now. It's…it's…"

"A god state," Blas said.

"Yeah. And the changes are happening fast. Talks about changing how men are ranked. Remember I shared that with you?"

"Ranked?" Blas said. "Don't pay attention to any of that. Just keep your head held high and do good."

"But they're watching everything. Just to get here was a battle," Pascal said.

"Then be prepared to fight," Blas said. "But that doesn't mean with violence."

"I know. No violence." Pascal shifted in his chair, straightened his posture.

"So, Dad, I wanted to share something with you."

"Whas it is, hijo?"

"I'm going to ask Tina to marry—well, you know, to make a commitment."

"That's great, hijo. Is this what you want? Is it what she wants?" Blas said.

"Well, yeah. We've been together for more than two years."

"You're already committed to each other," Blas said.

"Yes, that's why we're not going to call it marriage. But it will be tricky, with the marriage laws now. Domestic partnerships are frowned on. Having children out of an official marriage is an even bigger offense," Pascal said.

"Children?" Blas grabbed his son's shoulder, smiling. "See, you two are already committed if you're talking about children."

"Yeah, one of these days," Pascal smiled.

"Then you'll be just fine. Just do what your heart wants, okay?" Blas said.

"I always admired how you and mom did that, even when you knew your relationship was changing. When you two were changing."

"That's how families work," Blas said. "They change, and you're supposed to let them. If people didn't change, then I'd be worried."

"That's another thing I wanted to share. Or at least talk to you about," Pascal said.

Blas looked at him, waiting.

"I want to start. I want to be a healer, like you," Pascal said.

Blas's face twisted up. He bit his lip to fight his tears, but he let go, let them flow.

"I'm happy for you. I'm happy for us," Blas gripped his son's hand.

"Thanks, pa."

"But you know what, hijo? You're already a medicine man. You know the plants already."

"I think I do."

"I know you do. Now you just have to work on what needs healing within you," Blas said.

"That's why I'm here. I want to commune with the medicine and let go of my worries and problems. All my fears for the future, all my ghosts," Pascal said.

"You'll do that here. With all these gringos," Blas laughed again. "By the third day, you might be questioning your choices."

"You'll help me," Pascal said.

"She'll help you. Madre Ayahuasca." Blas reached over and placed his hand on Pascal's heart.

"How long are you going to stay here? In Peru?" Pascal said.

"As long as it takes," Blas said.

"As long as what takes?"

"As long as there are people coming to take the medicine. They can't do it there, so they come here," Blas said.

"I wish they could take it there," Pascal said.

"It's not time," Blas said. "That's where you come in."

"What do you mean?"

"I don't know. I think you're going to be part of that. You're going to help heal those lands once and for all," Blas said.

"How?"

"Do you remember when you and your sister were little and I would say that your jobs haven't been invented yet?" Blas said.

"Yeah?"

"Well, I'm going to say that again. Your job hasn't been invented yet. So, invent it."

Pascal looked out into the valley considering his father's words. The moon had risen and he didn't know what to say.

"I've heard they're trying to take the medicine," Blas said. "That is some news I keep up with."

Pascal turned to his father.

"You mean the retreat centers," he said. "There's one in Santa Fe. I was going to do a ceremony there."

"A ceremony." Blas smirked, pulled a coca leaf from the medicine box around his neck. He offered one to Pascal. "Those aren't ceremonies."

"No, they're not." Pascal took the leaf and followed his father's lead, who was now nibbling the leaf.

"They're the pharmaceutical industry stealing from the earth," Blas said.

"I spoke to one of their so-called shaman—" Pascal started, but Blas stopped him.

"Ya. Basta. They're nothing but thieves. Stay away. One day, you will bring it back the right way. The way of the ancestors. Now, let's rest. You are about to start a journey that will change you for the rest of your life," Blas said. "Tonight, as you drift off to sleep, I want you to ask any question or number of questions, but try to think of one. Concentrate on that one question. Ask anything. Big or small, past or present or future. About you, about humanity, the cosmos, anything. After a few days, after ceremony, you will have your answer loud and clear. All will come to you. Have no fear. What is meant for you, will come. What is not, will go away. Accept with ease, let go with ease."

Then, Blas put the tip of his index finger between his son Pascal's eyes, on the bridge of his nose.

"In due time," Blas said, gently tapping his son's nose. "En hora buena."

ONCE, A MAN

Once,
I was a rabbit
Innocent
Cute
Occasionally
Mischievous

Then,
I turned into a spider
Intelligent
Patient
Alone
In my delicate webs

Later,
I became a dog
Playful, trainable
Dutiful, beautiful
Annoyingly loyal

Now,
I am a bird

Skillful
Intuitive
With wings, claws, and beak
Ready to fly
Away

Acknowledgements

Mil gracias to several lifelines and creative thought partners including: Jeremy Lawson for lighting some fire under me to bring this to life, Scott Mitchell for always picking up the phone no matter the time and for continuing our lifelong conversation, Rodolfo Rivera Gaona for your brotherhood, guidance, and teaching, and to Kathyrn Wilson for your incredible insights and wisdom. Special thanks to Jess Walter for your continued mentorship.

Love and thank you to Summer Stewart at Unsolicited Press: your faith in my writing is a life blessing. To Kathryn Gerhardt, thank you for seeing the vision and your fine artistry.

About the Author

Taylor García is the author of the novel *Slip Soul,* and several short stories and essays. He also writes the weekly column, "Father Time" at the Good Men Project, and holds an MFA from Pacific University Oregon. García is a multi-generational Neomexicano originally from Santa Fé, New Mexico now living in Southern California with his wife and children.

About the Press

Unsolicited Press is based out of Portland, Oregon and focuses on the works of the unsung and underrepresented. As a womxn-owned, all-volunteer small publisher that doesn't worry about profits as much as championing exceptional literature, we have the privilege of partnering with authors skirting the fringes of the lit world. We've worked with emerging and award-winning authors such as Shann Ray, Amy Shimshon-Santo, Brook Bhagat, Kris Amos, and John W. Bateman.

Learn more at unsolicitedpress.com. Find us on twitter and instagram.